LITTLE BLUE ENCYCLOPEDIA

(for Vivian)

LITTLE BLUE ENCYCLOPEDIA

(for Vivian)

HAZEL JANE PLANTE

METONYMY PRESS

Montreal, Quebec

First edition
Second printing – 2020
Printed and bound in Canada by Imprimerie Gauvin
Interior and cover illustrations by Onjana Yawnghwe
Cover design by LOKI

Published by Metonymy Press
PO Box 143 BP Saint Dominique
Montreal, QC H2S 3K6
Canada
metonymypress.com

We acknowledge the support of the Canada Council for the Arts. Nous remercions le Conseil des arts du Canada de son soutien.

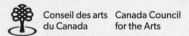

Library and Archives Canada Cataloguing in Publication

Title: Little blue encyclopedia : (for Vivian) / Hazel Jane Plante.
Names: Plante, Hazel Jane, author.
Identifiers: Canadiana (print) 20190166665 | Canadiana (ebook) 20190166681
| ISBN 9780994047199
   (softcover) | ISBN 9781999058814 (ebook)
Classification: LCC PS8631.L345 L58 2019 | DDC 813/.6—dc23

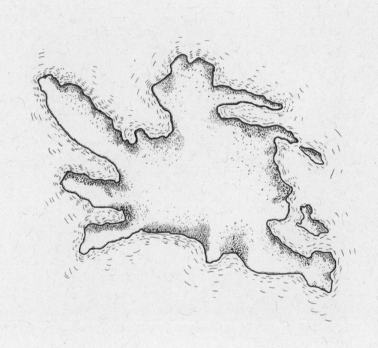

This book is about *Little Blue*, a television series that's adored by a small cluster of people. One of its keenest devotees was my friend Vivian Cloze. Like the series itself, she was enigmatic, flawed, and well loved. This book is as much about Vivian as it is about *Little Blue*.

When Vivian died, my world collapsed. I wept for what felt like days, weeks, months. Everything and everyone around me receded. Objects blurred. Colours drained. Sounds muffled.

Vivian was my favourite person. Intelligent. Beautiful. Ferocious. Charismatic. Open.

Her sister Dot asked me to help clear Vivian's belongings from her apartment. Dot found a babysitter for her son Teddy, and we worked our way through Viv's things. Some furniture, a sewing machine. A wardrobe that included several pieces she had hand tailored. A beloved bicycle, an ancient laptop. A stereo, a television. A small pile of books, a small collection of albums and films.

Dot had hoped to find some childhood photos among Viv's things, but we didn't unearth any. She took her sister's sewing machine and a handful of toys Viv had kept on hand for when Teddy visited. Her furniture went to her room-mate Claudia. We gave her robin's-egg-blue bike to a mutual friend who lived nearby. Her stylish shoes and boots went to her friend Tessa. We fit the rest of her things into boxes. Dot put most of them in the storage locker for her apartment. I filled a few boxes with things I wanted to go through when I had more energy, promising Dot she could have them when-ever she wanted.

Silently sifting through the remnants Viv had left in her wake felt like a sad dream. Dot was bleary eyed. I was bleary eyed. Viv was dead.

I never understood why Viv gravitated towards me. We only had a few things in common, but from the moment we met, we spent a lot of time together. The guys she dated would get jealous, send text messages with emojis of egg-plants and cats with heart eyes.

Sometimes we would hang out in Viv's apartment, play-ing video games. Claudia was rarely around. When she was home, she typically stayed in her room. Claudia occasion-ally surprised me by appearing in the kitchen to make her-self a pot of tea. She always seemed sheepish and apologetic, even though we were the ones inconveniencing her. Mostly, Viv and I would wander around town, talking. When we got tired of walking and talking, we'd find a bench. If it was rainy, we'd carry umbrellas. She thought best when she walked; I thought best when I was around her. I always felt more artic-ulate talking to Viv. I was fuelled by coffee; she worked in a coffee shop, but didn't get caffeine, claimed it had no effect on her. She'd bring a travel cup filled with one uncaffeinated beverage or another. We talked about everything under the sky. After a while, I realized she didn't want to talk about her past. I talked quite a bit about my younger self, but I always sensed that she wanted me to follow her lead and let it all fall away. She'd crossed a border and the past was now a country that she no longer wanted to visit.

I took her to the art gallery once for a sprawling exhibition called *European Paint, North American Paint*. In the European painters section, she drifted past still lifes by Cézanne and Monet, gravitating instead towards more playful and abstract works by Klee and Miró. In the North American painters area, she lingered in front of a vast canvas covered in swirls and streaks of red paint. It was bright and messy and the paint was thickly layered. After a while, she sat on a bench across from the painting. I sat down beside her. We sat silently for a few minutes and I tried to appreciate the painting, but it didn't do much for me. I asked her what she saw in it. She bit her lip and scrunched her eyes. After a longish pause, she said, "I don't know. It's got an energy. If it were a different colour or a different size, I don't know how I'd feel about it. But the way it towers over me and fills my eyes with red … I don't know. The other stuff here is okay, I guess. But this one does something. It's like a giant red door. Or a giant wound. Or a giant angry cunt." I'm sure that I blushed at this point because, well, she'd said the word "cunt" and we were in an art gallery. We were already a conspicuous pair wherever we went. She was on a swearing roll, though, and said the painting was "just so fucking brilliant." When I asked who the artist was, she shrugged. I was used to people largely gauging how much they liked art based on the prestige of the artist, rather than just looking at the work. Even the crappiest Picasso always had a gaggle of people leaning in to inspect the brushstrokes,

3

whereas an amazing work by a lesser-known painter would generally get a cursory glance.

I walked over to the looming painting and read its label:

Beulah Holmstrom
American, 1914–1987

Red No. 42, 1966
Oil and blood on canvas

On loan from the Art Institute of Chicago

Beulah Holmstrom is associated with the abstract expressionists and color field painters. She gradually narrowed her palette to include only shades of red, a development one prominent art critic declared "signals she has lost her artistic bearings and is sending flares of emergency red in the darkness, casting a pall on gallery walls."

Red No. 42 is significant in Holmstrom's development as an artist because the canvas includes the first use of her menstrual blood. At the time, she didn't divulge the inclusion of blood as one of the materials in her work. This information was discovered in her notebooks several years after her death and the presence of blood was confirmed by analyzing her paintings. She has been cited as an influence by many contemporary artists.

When I told Viv, her eyes lit up. "She used her own menstrual blood?! That's genius!" While I appreciated the idea, I still wasn't sure about her work. That's when Viv first mentioned

Little Blue. I remember because I was confused by the name and thought she was talking about colours. After a few sentences, I had lost the conversational map. I interrupted her and she realized that I'd never seen *Little Blue*, which disappointed and thrilled her. A day or two later, we started watching the television series together.

Watching *Little Blue* with Vivian was peculiar because I could tell she was often watching me while I was watching the television. She never said a word, but the weight of her attention was palpable. It was endearing how badly she wanted me to finish watching all ten episodes. After watching a couple back to back, I'd beg off, but she'd always convince me to watch another one. It became a weird potato chip thing of always needing to have just one more, but it was like she was force feeding me potato chips. Sure, I was happy to nibble on chips, but I didn't want to eat chips for three or four hours in a row. Viv was adamant that we couldn't discuss anything about the show until I'd seen every episode, so she was urging me to watch all ten hours of the series. Her fervour to discuss the show was bubbling over. I'd be walking to the front door to put on my raincoat and boots, saying goodbye, and she'd be pretending to nibble on a handful of potato chips.

"Nom nom nom nom."

"Sorry, Viv, I've gotta go."

"Nom nom nom. I love these chips! Nom nom."

"I've got to get up early tomorrow."

"Mmm! Salt 'n' vinegar! Nom nom."

"Bye!"

Watching *Little Blue* for the first time was bananas. So many characters. So much quirk. A character who speaks Danish without subtitles. A character who sings rather than speaks. A secret diorama. Pigeon racing. An entire episode devoted to baseball. A subplot about two people being murdered by someone wearing a bear costume. This was Viv's favourite television show? Maybe *Red No. 42* wasn't so bad after all.

When the tenth episode ended, my head felt as foggy as the windows of a car in mid-winter. Viv assumed I'd be befuddled. Watching it for the first time is always an overwhelming experience. So, she started by focussing on just one character. Roy Spittle.

Roy is an abstract painter who works with a limited palette. When we first see him, he is painting with the colours indigo, violet, and yellow as an ongoing visual eulogy for his wife, Ivy Elder, who died in a boating accident. Prior to her death, he was painting with a palette of colours derived from his own name: red, orange, and yellow. Perhaps Viv had been primed to appreciate *Red No. 42* through her repeated exposure to Roy Spittle's paintings on *Little Blue*. It didn't hurt that she tended towards abstraction, arguing that art that tried to capture life through realism always fell short. *Little Blue* certainly didn't aim for realism. It was a wonky layer cake of ideas. But it was delightfully wonky and Viv always appreciated anything that tilted towards delight. She claimed to have made many major decisions by asking herself which option available to her might result in the most delight.

When Viv spoke of *Little Blue*, her description resembled what I'd seen, but it was far more coherent. I vaguely remembered most of the people and events that she mentioned, partly because I'd watched the entire series in the short span of a few days, but it had been impossible to connect the dots in the ways that she could. *Little Blue* had a density that I'd never encountered outside of particularly challenging novels, but with novels you can turn back a few pages to refresh your memory, which isn't as easy to do with a television series.

Roy Spittle had a daughter, Pauline Elder, who had been named for Ivy Elder's kindly father, Paul, who died with Ivy on the boat, along with his wife, Marjorie. Roy and Pauline had a three-legged Beagle named Visconti.

Roy is one of the first characters we meet in *Little Blue*. Two strangers take a ferry to Little Blue Island, where Roy runs Little Blue RV Park, which he took over managing after Ivy's tragic death. Roy frequents Little Blue Diner, where he sips coffee, snacks on pastries, and talks to his closest friend, Dalton Fludd, a poet who drives a tugboat. Roy confesses to Dalton that he still sees Ivy in his dreams regularly.

I was amazed to realize how closely and frequently Viv had watched *Little Blue*. She seemed to know every-thing about every character, including things that were only glimpsed for a second or two or weren't even shown onscreen. It was like going for a walk through the woods with an arborist, who not only identifies every species of tree around you, but also shares unexpected tidbits about them. In fact, one of Viv's favourite characters on *Little Blue*, Agnes Pennypacker, is an arborist, who does just that during a nature walk with another character.

Over time, I came to love *Little Blue*. I didn't love it as deeply as Viv, but her enthusiasm infected me with a benign little blue parasite that made me want to rewatch the series regularly. Before Viv died, I never rewatched the series on my own; my particular parasite made me crave watching it with Viv. If you're wondering if parasites appear in *Little Blue*, you'll be pleased to know that yes, they do.

One aspect of *Little Blue* that Vivian related to was its abundance of absent characters, including Ivy Elder. Viv lost so many people when she told them she was trans: all of her relatives (except her sister), most of her close friends, and her boyfriend. She didn't like to talk about her life before she transitioned, but Dot told me later that their parents did everything they could to "fix" Viv. When she left for university and transitioned, her parents refused to call her by her name and use female pronouns. Eventually, she couldn't endure being unseen and unaccepted, so she cut off contact with them. (A sad coda to their relationship: When Vivian died, Dot ran an obituary in two newspapers, including the paper in their hometown. Her parents immediately contacted the newspaper to demand that it run a retraction and publish a new obituary with her deadname and male pronouns, which the paper refused to do.)[1]

When Vivian died, I stopped going to grad school. She was the person who'd persuaded me to go back to school and study journalism. With her gone, I saw no point in doing meaningless assignments like writing an advertorial on a tech start-up. The one time I did force myself to go to class (well, I was peer pressured into showing up for a group assignment), I muddled through my portion of a presentation on how to best "leverage" a new social media platform for journalism. When class ended, the prof asked me if we could have a brief chat. She'd missed me in class the previous week. Plus, my mascara had started to run. I'd curse my drugstore mascara, but it probably saved me from a life of crime. Okay, that might be overdoing it. I can say that if my prof

---

1   A note to journalists: There is rarely a good reason to print a trans person's deadname. If it's to tell your readers what their previous name was—or to tell them what their "real name" is—that is not a good reason. If you deadname me in my obituary, I will fuck you up. Seriously. I have a contingency plan in place if this happens. It will be Armageddon, trans style. ;)

hadn't stopped me after class that day, I may have dropped out of grad school. She convinced me to take a leave of absence, get my psychic shit together, and return when I was strong enough to finish my degree. My heart hurt when she said there weren't enough trans writers, a point Viv had also stressed when she convinced me to finally apply to the program. I dotted all the official i's and crossed all the official t's to take a break from grad school.

What do you think I did with my time away from school? Reconnect with friends and family? Volunteer? Meditate? Go for long walks along the water? None of the above. I worked just enough hours in the gift store at the art gallery to pay for food and rent. When I wasn't working, I slept and ate and mimed a life.

After a few months of emptiness and anger, I felt the urge to sift through the boxes in my closet that held remnants of Vivian. The first box I opened contained a tailored houndstooth trench coat that she adored. I tried it on. It was a little snug, but I felt good in it. Standing in the coat, I felt so intensely that Vivian was still alive, somehow. I imagined a hummingbird trapped inside my heart, its tiny wings vibrating against my rib cage. I imagined it quivering and expanding and, finally, folding in on itself. I put my hands in the coat pockets, where I found an old tube of lip gloss. Viv was a fiend for lip gloss.

Beneath the trench coat, the box held a small collection of albums, books, and DVDs. I removed an album that I recognized and put it on my turntable. *Different Class* by Pulp. A year or so ago, Vivian had sung its opening song "Mis-Shapes" at karaoke. She couldn't really sing, but she was mesmerizing and impassioned and sang to our table, which was surrounded by half a dozen trans women. It felt like she was singing a defiant anthem that had been written specifically for us. I was astounded at how easily she could carry the room, even if she couldn't carry a tune. When the song ended, she came back to our table, spent and smiling. "Holy fuck, do I love all of you," she said. She went around and gave each of us a long, slow hug. That may have been the night I realized how much I loved her.

As the song played on my turntable, I suddenly heard the jubilant line about how "the future is owned by you and me" and it hit me like a rabbit punch. The future was no longer owned by Vivian. She only had a past. My vision blurred. I wiped away tears with the houndstooth sleeve. I removed the album from the turntable and slid it into its cover. As I was putting it back in the box, I spotted the DVD box set for *Little Blue*. At that moment, I wanted more than anything to cozy up on the couch beside Viv and rewatch the series. I pulled the discs out and put them aside to revisit later. As I was closing the box, my eyes were drawn to a tattered children's encyclopedia. Viv had cherished this book and I never knew why. It had something to do with her child-hood, I assumed. I put the encyclopedia beside the discs for *Little Blue*. Maybe Dot could shed some light on the mystery behind this book. It was like a Nancy Drew title: *The Secret of the Tattered Encyclopedia*. Everything else went back in the closet, except for the trench coat, which retained a hint of Vivian's citrusy perfume and would prove useful for sopping up stray tears.

A few days later, Dot had me over for one of Viv's favou-rite dishes, vegetarian lasagne. Getting together every couple of weeks was one of the ways that we helped each other to cope. Dot had stopped breastfeeding recently and was drinking again, so we would normally have wine with dinner. Once we tried to watch one of Viv's favourite screw-ball comedies, but Teddy was particularly rambunctious, so we abandoned it. When we were together, Dot and I hugged a lot. Teddy would join in on the hugs, which was lovely. I was happy to be his honorary auntie, but he deserved to get to know his Aunt Vivian. She loved Teddy so much.

Teddy ate his lasagne with a side of sliced apples and strawberries. He wore the FUTURE FEMINIST bib I'd bought for him. After dinner, Dot managed to get Teddy to sleep and we sat on the side of the couch not strewn with toys, talking about Vivian and how we were both doing. We drank more wine. I noticed the letters *enc* scrawled on my hand and remembered the encyclopedia. I fished the worn book from my handbag. Dot recognized it immediately. It had been a gift from a relative when they were growing up. Their parents refused to buy her and Viv books because they thought they were things you only used once and discarded, like the rind of an orange. As a result, the encyclopedia was one of the only books in their shared bedroom. Soon, Viv had stuck stickers throughout the encyclopedia wherever there was blank space. After that, Dot let her have the book, though she recalled later taking possession of a single volume from an encyclopedia set the same relative gave them. That volume only covered half of the letter **A**, but she gamely tried reading it from cover to cover. Even now, she could recall poring over pages on abalone, airmail, Albania, and anchors. She claimed to have found the illustrations of anchors especially memorable. I told her that one of my favourite necklaces of Viv's had an anchor pendant. Unsurprisingly, Viv had borrowed the necklace from Dot years ago and never returned it.

I'd initially bonded with Dot when I gave her an olive-green cardigan that I'd knitted for newborn Teddy. She loved it. Viv was surprised that I could knit. After that, I had come over every few weeks to knit with Dot. She was working on a sweater for Teddy with an Icelandic pattern, but it was going slowly. I would get anxious because I wondered if it was going to fit Teddy when she eventually finished it. But she had already anticipated that it would take her quite a while to knit the sweater. When she finally put it on Teddy, it looked incredible and was appropriately loose. Dot is one smart cookie.

We started flipping through Viv's encyclopedia. It briefly covered every topic from aardvarks to zooplankton. There were colourful drawings throughout and each page had a tiny drawing of a squid that surrounded the number of the page you were on. It seemed weird until I remembered that it was called the *Squid Encyclopedia for Kids*. Squid was the name of the publisher.

Dot told me that Viv had gone through a phase when she was about ten of trying to memorize the entire book, one letter of the alphabet per week. She only kept it up for a few weeks. Dot said her sister was a whiz at geography, but she struggled to remember esoteric trivia about states, including state birds and sales-tax rates. After abandoning her goal of memorizing the book, she traced nearly every one of its maps. Then, she started drawing her own maps for imaginary countries. Apparently, she became fixated at one point on an imaginary archipelago called the Sassafras Islands. Dot didn't know why her sister glommed on to the word "sassafras" but it was one that Viv seemed to adore. She even told Dot that Sassafras was her secret name. I thought it sounded quite femme and Dot agreed. At the time, she thought Viv liked the word because it was fun to say and it had the word "ass" in it twice.

On the "male" reproductive system illustration in the encyclopedia, Viv had placed stickers of colourful flowers over the figure's penis, glans penis, foreskin, testis, scrotum, and epididymis. When we came across that altered page, I looked at Dot, who had a faint, pained smile. "I miss her so much," Dot whispered. I nodded and wrapped my arms around her.

As we were saying goodbye, I told Dot that I was planning to rewatch *Little Blue*. She laughed and shook her head. "Well, good luck with that," she said. "Even V couldn't convince me to finish watching it. Totally confusing and totally batshit." I once asked Viv's roommate Claudia if she'd ever watched *Little Blue* and she gave me a look of mild panic and said that she'd tried to watch it, but it wasn't for her. Clearly, Viv had tried and failed to indoctrinate her shy roommate.

When I started rewatching *Little Blue*, I had to re-adapt to its overabundance and disjointedness. I was reminded of something a television critic had once said that gets quoted regularly on websites and articles devoted to *Little Blue*: "Jason Bloch [the show's creator] is to television what Stockhausen was to music: a disruptive force who expands our options." It's a supersaturated substance. It's a Dagwood sandwich. It's an athlete who literally gives 200 percent. *Little Blue* crams twenty hours of material into ten hour-long episodes. Once I became reacclimated to its jarring swiftness and too-much-ness, I settled into a routine that included watching a couple of episodes a day.

At the same time, I'd started jotting down my memories of Vivian. There was so much about her that I knew might be forgotten if I didn't try to preserve it. I didn't want her to disappear from this world, unremembered and unseen. She deserved so much more. Plus, I told myself that I was still a fledgling journalist and needed to write about something, so I should write about what I cared about more than anything. Rewatching *Little Blue* reminded me of so many small things about Viv. The series is sprawling, so even a single episode could trigger a cascade of memories. After watching all ten, I'd loop back to the first episode. Lather, rinse, repeat.

After a few weeks of cycling through the series, my brother Christopher and a couple of friends worried that I was spending too much time deep within the rabbit hole of *Little Blue*, but I knew that its safety and warmth weren't at odds with the bobbing and weaving of daily life. Art can distract and soothe and mend. I still felt numb and stunned by Viv's death, but watching *Little Blue* was like spending a couple of hours a night with the peculiar residents of a small island, snuggled up on the couch beside Viv's ghost and my sleepy tortoiseshell cat, Whisk.

I wish I could say that writing about Viv and watching her favourite series served as a sort of emotional spackle that helped to partially fill the painful gap in my life that appeared when she died, but it wasn't like that. Watching *Little Blue* with her imagined ghost wasn't like being with her. Writing about her wasn't like being with her. There was a strange, bittersweet beauty to thinking deeply about Viv every day, but the truth is it only made me more acutely aware that she was gone, that her thoughts were gone, her words were gone, her body was gone. I became increasingly aware of my body, of all the things I had done in it and all the things I could do in it. Viv was more attuned to her body than most people. You can see this in photos of her. She's always positioned gracefully even when she didn't know she was being photographed, whereas I'm often slouching or tilting my head or holding my hands awkwardly.

I'd already filled a few small notebooks with memories of her. Her encyclopedia was always nearby and I'd occasionally flip through it, picking up a few stray outdated facts. One day, I turned to the **V** section. After all, **V** is for Vivian.

I looked closely at the maps for Venezuela and Vietnam. She appeared to have lightly traced Venezuela, but the map for Vietnam seemed to have been traced multiple times. She had also jotted marginalia in the entries for video games and volcanos. The video-game jottings consisted of a list of contemporary games that weren't mentioned in the entry. She'd also placed stickers of a few of her favourite video-game characters in the margins.

I hadn't really thought about what I'd do with the fragments about Viv that I was writing, if anything. Now I wondered if I should try arranging them around the alphabet. It seemed like an arbitrary structure, but one that felt more interesting and closer to her than something more straightforward and linear. She tended to ricochet from this thing to that thing before you could bat an eyelash. I spent a few days combing through what I'd written, circling passages that I liked and putting a tentative word beside them for where they might appear in the alphabetical list of entries. Once that was accomplished, I wanted to see how they would fit together. Perhaps this structure was just as confusing and batshit as Dot found *Little Blue*. Rather than transcribing the entries into my computer, I unearthed Viv's ancient laptop. It still worked and didn't prompt me for a password.

It took longer than anticipated to transcribe, rearrange, and edit the alphabetical entries. When I finally read the rough draft, it was shambolic as fuck. It leapfrogged from subject to subject, kept alluding to *Little Blue*, and worst of all, the Viv I knew was entirely absent from what I'd written. I'd spent so many hours trying to convey something about Viv, and I'd failed.

I got up, paced, and sat back down. Whisk gave me a lazy look from her scratching post by the window. She had one of her paws dangling over the edge. I took a deep breath and wondered what Viv would do. My first thought was that she would pour herself a drink. If some especially important thinking needed to be done, she might pour herself two or three fingers of Chartreuse. Unlike Viv, I didn't have any lovers who bought me Chartreuse, so I poured myself a tall gin and tonic. I sipped it and pondered how I could salvage what I'd written.

I walked over to my bookshelf and gathered a handful of my favourite nonfiction titles. Maybe one of them would suggest a way forward. The first two books had conventional, linear structures. The third book was a different species entirely. It was a memoir by Maritime artist Chase Abernathy called *An Illustrated History of My Pants*. The book has an unusual format because after its initial eighty pages of autobiography, you discover a hollowed-out section, like you'd see in a book that's meant to hold your valuables or a concealed weapon. Instead, the hollow area in the memoir contains twenty-six objects:

› Five old photographs
› Ten small reproductions of drawings
› Ten small booklets
› One swatch of burgundy corduroy fabric

As its title suggests, the small illustrations in *An Illustrated History of My Pants* depict pairs of pants Chase has owned. The ten slender booklets feature stories related to the ten pairs of pants in the small drawings. The old photographs show five skirts from Chase's childhood. They are not mentioned in the text and the memoir starts with Chase arriving as a twenty-two-year-old butch artist to study at the Nova Scotia College of Art and Design.

On paper, the book may sound gimmicky. In your hands, it is something to behold, an impressive nest of papery art objects. The book was a gift from Ramona, my girlfriend at the time. We'd met at an exhibit of Chase's work. I was jotting notes in a notebook for a review of the exhibit for my university's student newspaper. Ramona was standing nearby, sketching in her sketchbook. I glanced over and saw that she was sketching *Bras d'Or*, which is a large door that has been entirely covered in pointy brass bras. Where the doorknob should be, a slender, alabaster arm protrudes with its palm open in a classic "stop" gesture, keeping the viewer at a distance. The piece somehow merges the Middle Ages with Blond Ambition–era Madonna, the sacred and the sacrilegious. Ramona managed to capture the feel of the work in her rough sketch. She saw me looking at her sketchbook and reddened. "I didn't quite get it," she said, "but this is raddest door I've ever seen. I mean, spiky bras and a handle that doesn't want to be handled? The best!" I smiled. It was a pretty rad door. We introduced ourselves and discovered we were both studying art at different universities, visual art for her and art history for me. We started dating and moved in together a few months later. For my birthday, she gave me a copy of *An Illustrated History of My Pants*, which was published in a limited edition of 260 copies, each of them numbered and signed by Chase Abernathy. I was overwhelmed. This was a thoughtful, pricey gift, and I knew she didn't make much at her part-time job in a consignment clothing store. For her birthday, I had vague plans of treating her to chicken and waffles and getting her a cute pair of rain boots because her current pair had started splitting apart at the ankles.

I was as fascinated by Chase's identity as his subversive art. He identified variously as butch, a "gender upender," and trans. At the same time, his work was often steeped in feminine imagery, like the brass bra–covered door in *Bras d'Or* or its companion piece, a diptych called *Lake*. *Lake* was a painted map of Bras d'Or Lake, located in Cape Breton, Nova Scotia. The lake was bisected, with half of it painted on the left panel of the diptych and the other half painted on the right panel. The lake on the left canvas was labelled with the names of locations that dot the shore of Bras d'Or Lake. Lime Hill. West Alba. Malagawatch. Red Point. Plaster Cove. The lake on the right canvas was labelled with parts of a vulva. Labia Majora. Labia Minora. Clitoris. Urethral Opening. Vagina. If you look at a map of Bras d'Or Lake, you have to admit that it is more pussy shaped than most lakes.

For some reason, I never mentioned Chase Abernathy's art to Vivian. She would have particularly loved his painting *Chebucto Head*. It's a sprawling, Bosch-like depiction of consensual debauchery. The work is startling in its level of detail, leaving no sexual act unrepresented. It's awash in wanton tongues, lips, teeth, fingers, cunts, cocks, tits, asses, and slippery bodily fluids. The painting became infamous because it was mentioned by name when Chase Abernathy was denounced by a contingent of Conservative members of Parliament as a "taxpayer-funded pornographer" because he had received a Canada Council for the Arts grant that year. Even worse, he was referred to as a "highly controversial female-to-male transgendered artist who peddles smut subsidized by innocent Canadian families." He was also deadnamed in Parliament and in articles written on the controversy. He responded by commissioning a local company to produce a handful of one-of-a-kind dildos that featured the warped faces of the Conservative politicians who had denounced and deadnamed him. He titled the piece *If You Can't Stay Out of My Ass* and its museum label listed the artisanal dildos' materials as "medical-grade silicone and artist's fecal residue."

In *An Illustrated History of My Pants*, Chase includes a

drawing of the leather pants he wore "that night on Chebucto Head when I discovered in a beat-up red truck that bodies can be as succulent as ripe fruit." He goes on to say that in the cramped quarters of the truck he "finally understood that lovers are shameless cartographers of skin and pleasure." In a description that Viv would have appreciated, he states even more nakedly that he painted *Chebucto Head* to commemorate "the most delicious fuck of my life."

Anyway.

While paging through *An Illustrated History of My Pants*, I started to recognize how many of my memories of Vivian were entwined with *Little Blue*. We spent so many hours together watching it, discussing it, quoting it. While writing about Viv, I'd found myself unable to avoid drawing connections to her life and *Little Blue*'s colourful characters. Agnes Pennypacker. Sherman Park. Chet Tully. May Underwood. These names carry a resonance that's impossible to convey if you're unfamiliar with *Little Blue*, sort of like reeling off the evocative names of kids you knew in elementary school. I'm never going to write about my childhood classmates, but I knew I'd need to write about the characters from *Little Blue* to write about Viv.

One night while drinking red wine and listening to music, I found myself gazing absently at Viv's *Little Blue* DVDs and *Squid Encyclopedia for Kids* on my weathered writing desk. They were stacked on top of one another. It was a classic peanut-butter-meets-jelly moment. Suddenly, writing an encyclopedia about *Little Blue* steeped in memories of Vivian made perfect sense. I opened Viv's laptop and created a fresh document called *Little Blue Encyclopedia*. That title didn't look quite right, so I added *(for Vivian)*.

This book is the closest you'll get to knowing my favourite person and it's the closest you'll get to watching *Little Blue*

with her, which was a delightful experience.
I miss you so fucking much, Viv.

Captain ALPHONSE abandoned his wife and child the day after his son spoke his first word. We never see any images of Alphonse, nor do we discover his family name, what he was "captain" of, or (most importantly) why he left his wife and young son. Captain Alphonse is described either vaguely or contradictorily. When someone says "He was the real deal" with no other information, what does that mean? And how can you be "a man's man to beat the band" and have the nickname Twinkle Toes? Was the nickname meant to be a joke, like calling a large kid Tiny? Somehow, he managed to captivate Ranjit Jha, the most beautiful woman on Little Blue

Island, who continued to love him even after he abandoned her and their child, Tristan.

In the character of Captain Alphonse, I get a whiff of what Vivian was attracted to in men: an airy charm, a greasy charisma. And good hair. I'm sure Captain Alphonse had good hair, as well as a handsome face and an opaque expression. Viv had a thing for drummers with doe eyes. Maybe a certain kind of woman finds it hard to resist guys dripping with machismo and musk.

Charles ("Chappy") AMBLESIDE purchased Little Blue Island as a young man and tried to extract minerals from it, only to discover that the quantities and types of minerals to be found were not valuable enough to make mining worthwhile. As a result, he sold plots of stolen land to settlers. He became the self-proclaimed Emperor of Cucumbers using cultivation techniques robbed from the island's most successful settler, Toshiro Tanake, after Tanake and his family were sent to an internment camp during World War II. His whispered final words are said to have been either "All kneel before the Emperor of Cucumbers" or "I see before me the terror of endless slumber." He left his cucumber empire to his son, Roderick.

"Half Bloomer" AMBLESIDE is Roderick Ambleside's daughter. She is a quiet and guarded child. Throughout the *Little Blue* series, she only says two words aloud: "yes" and "no." She seems to love ducks, gum, and origami.

Roderick AMBLESIDE, Little Blue Island's self-proclaimed soda tycoon, owns most of the island, including the cucumber operation, a soda company, a general store, and a pub. His preferred mode of travel on the small island is helicopter.

Roderick appears to have lured a renowned astronomer to the island to secure his own legacy by having a star discovered and named after him. Right after inheriting his father's fortune, he was swindled by a carpenter who disappeared with a sizeable sum after being commissioned to build him a spiral staircase with 10,000 stairs. Shortly thereafter, he rebounded and started the Little Blue Soda Company.

I can't resist drawing parallels between Vivian's troubled relationship with her father and the dynamic between "Half Bloomer" and Roderick Ambleside. Viv rarely mentioned her upbringing, but the things I heard later from Dot were heartbreaking. Their father had a nickname for Viv that was far worse than "Half Bloomer." I won't repeat it and wish I'd never heard it. But there's a value in knowing what Viv had to endure because it makes her open-heartedness that much more astonishing. She had every reason to protect herself with character armour and curl up in a ball like a little femme armadillo, but she remained vulnerable and open. When she fell for a new guy, she would be a cute bundle of generosity and trust, even though she'd been hurt by people all her life. I told her more than once that she was naive, that men are the worst, that they're not to be trusted, that we'd both been behind the curtain and heard them saying things they'd never knowingly say in front of women. She knew all of this, but it didn't dissolve her attraction to men. She once texted me about seeing someone on transit reading a book about how to be in love without being vulnerable. She was incredulous that people would think you could be in love and remain bulletproof.

She added in her typical staccato texting style:
if you love someone, you expose yourself
your tender spots
you have to

you want to
you might regret it
but you dive in
DON'T YOU?

Mr. BITS is the charismatic, alcoholic high school English teacher. He'd been an all-star pitcher while he was a student at Little Blue School. He left the island on a baseball scholarship and became a top prospect for baseball scouts as a pitcher in college. While pitching a no-hitter in a championship game, he suddenly became unable to throw the ball accurately. He hit three batters in a row and was pulled from the game. He failed to regain his throwing accuracy and was cut from the team. He sank into depression, started drinking, and returned to Little Blue Island to teach at his old high school.

The fourth episode of *Little Blue* is contentious, even among fans of the show. Its opening credits resemble what we would expect at the start of a typical televised baseball game: shots of the field, the fans, and the starting lineups, which consist of characters from the series. Before we know it, Mr. Bits of the Little Blue Cubs is pitching to Chet Tully, leadoff batter for the Little Blue Bears. The game looks remarkably similar to any other broadcast baseball game with statistics for each player, slow-motion instant replays, and two announcers providing commentary.

When the episode first aired, many viewers were baffled and thought an actual baseball game was being broadcast in place of *Little Blue*. The local fictitious ads are also priceless, especially the one for Chet Tully's Chet the Baker home-made pastries with the absurd tagline "Chet makes your taste buddies high five!" The crude animation of two tongues high fiving makes me smile. Even though it's not one of my favourites, this episode includes some genius moments. And now I just want to hear Vivian laugh her laugh and give me an awkward high five. She had a massive crush on Chet Tully, the baker behind the Chet the Baker brand. Predictably, he was an asshole, but a handsome one.

Viv loved the looks of the sugar skull tattoo on Mr. Bits's left hand, the one that gave up the ghost mid-game and couldn't find the strike zone. The tattoo is only glimpsed a couple of times, but it looks phenomenal. She was tempted to get one done above her right nipple. She decided against it because she didn't like his character and, well, she didn't want to pilfer a symbol from Mexico's Día de Muertos that was intended to honour dead friends and relatives.

When a friend of hers died, Viv would get a small tattoo of their initials near her heart. I have an image on my phone of the flock of cursive lettering: JT. LD. AKG. I only knew

AKG, who was a high-maintenance barista from Moose Jaw with a sweet tooth and a lopsided grin.

Viv only had one other tattoo: the beautiful, scarred face and dramatic hair of the bride in *Bride of Frankenstein*. On more than one drunken occasion, Viv had quoted the monster in the final scene from *Bride of Frankenstein*: "We belong dead." After saying this line, a tear falls from the monster's eye, and he pulls a lever that triggers an explosion, destroying the castle and killing the bride and himself. We both admitted to feeling like monsters some of the time. If people question your right to exist, strangers give you stink eye, and men who kill trans women aren't held accountable, how can you not feel like there's something wrong with you or that the world wants you to disappear or die?

After Viv died, Dot revealed that her sister had tried to kill herself once. Viv had told me that the first person she confided in that she might be trans was someone she loved and trusted. That person stunned her by broadcasting this secret to everyone he could. She was devastated and went through a dark period. She likened it to paddling in a rowboat with a good friend who suddenly takes an oar and clubs you in the head with it, knocking you into the water, unconscious. You regain consciousness and find you're in the middle of the ocean, the boat is gone, and you don't know which way to paddle. You tread water. Your energy ebbs. Your head goes under the water. You come up again. As you bob in the water, on the verge of giving in and sinking down, you spot a bright light. You slowly inch along towards it, bobbing and pushing and, finally, making it to shore. What Viv hadn't told me was that she attempted suicide during the dark days after being betrayed by her friend. Hearing this story, I couldn't keep it together. Dot walked over and gave me a hug. She held me a long time.

I only have one tattoo: The letter **V** written in cursive above my heart. The tattoo artist based the design on the ornate **V** in Vivian's signature.

Leora BLEST is a volatile line cook at Little Blue Pub. It's refreshing to see an unabashedly angry woman on television, and Leora has a white-knuckled rage that simmers in nearly every one of her scenes. Her temper is only offset by her dream of opening a fine-dining establishment and her tender relationship with her lover, Louise Quince.

Viv loved that Leora's anger was never explained, so viewers had to interpret it. As with a Rorschach test, your interpretation of what you are seeing says more about you than about the thing you are interpreting. Her anger was captivating in a way that male aggression onscreen rarely seems to be. A red-headed soft butch dragon interacting with meek townsfolk. There's always a a coil-spring-ed-ness, something seething below the surface. And this tension only increases after we witness her going ballistic on Ian Earl Stairs. I have yet to meet anyone who's watched the show and not been gobsmacked by this moment.

Sadly, Leora is a lightning rod for some men. Don't try to defend Ian Earl Stairs's comment as harmless. And, no, she wouldn't be prettier if she smiled or if she had long hair or wore more makeup. And, yes, she does wear a lot of flannel.

Tycho BRAHE is Roderick Ambleside's gold-nosed personal astronomer, who rocks this cool "nü Viking" look. Tycho lost his original nose one dark night in a drunken duel to determine who was the better mathematician. When he discovers a new comet, he christens it the Underwood-Brahe Comet, which appears to prompt May Underwood to return to Tycho, who she'd left for her high school sweetheart.

Viv crushed on so many characters on *Little Blue*, but Tycho Brahe might be one of the only ones that made sense to me. He is beguiling and pouty, especially when he's pining for May. Plus, it's adorable that he speaks Danish and only knows a few phrases of English.

A complete list of every English phrase spoken by Tycho:

› "I am Tycho! Who are you?"
› "The pleasure is mine!"
› "Punk rock!"
› "More soda!"
› "Gimme candy!"
› "Denmark love the Danish!"

Viv and I often borrowed Tycho's rallying cry of "More soda!" It's such a simple, elastic phrase that can be used in almost any situation. "More TV!" "More wine!" "More cuddling!"

Newbies to *Little Blue* are often confused that other characters on the show understand what Tycho is saying, even though he's speaking Danish. The fact that there are no English subtitles when he speaks is another obstacle for some viewers. Complicating things further, it's also unclear whether he is meant to be the legendary sixteenth-century Danish astronomer Tycho Brahe, who has somehow travelled ahead in time, or if he is meant to be delusional.

After May Underwood breaks up with him, a montage oscillates between silent footage of Tycho binging on soda, candy, and pastries, and deafening clips of him blasting punk rock in his castle while jumping on his Scandinavian furniture, windmilling on an air guitar, and headbanging.

Dot once told me she was a punker when she was younger. I was surprised because I'd seen photos of her growing up and she didn't dress like I thought a punker would dress. She felt that if you were truly punk, you didn't need to dress punk.

"Punk wasn't about wearing bondage pants or Docs or whatever," she said. "It was a state of mind. Throughout high school, I lived on a steady diet of punk rock. The Raincoats. The Avengers. The Adverts. X-Ray Spex. For a while, I wanted so badly to hang out with the other punks at my high school. But I also thought they were poseurs with their mohawks, their leather jackets, and their safety pins. Because I didn't dress punk, I'm sure they thought I was the poseur." She shrugged. "Now that I'm older and less of a contrarian, I can admit that maybe I overthought being punk."

Viv wasn't a fan of most punk rock, a point of some friction when she and Dot were growing up. But she did love "My Vengeance" by the Wipers. It's the song that blares while Tycho channels his frustration and sadness by rocking out.

> So hard being a human being
> Controlled by the ways and the means
> Some people just give it up
> Fat chance
> My vengeance

These lyrics unfold in my mind like a palimpsest, where the phrase "give it up" is written over by the words "fat chance," which is then covered in spray paint with the defiant, similar-sounding phrase "my vengeance." Give up on life? I don't think so. In fact, I'll make you pay for trying to squish me like a caterpillar. Viv's vengeance was being a badass trans woman who made it clear that she belonged here as much as anyone. In public spaces, she was undaunted. Her vengeance was being resilient and resistant and alive.

"My Vengeance" knocks me sideways because Viv had endured so much and died long before she should have. And I suddenly remember her talking about receiving her new birth certificate. She didn't think it would matter. But in the nondescript envelope was a kind of official recognition that she didn't know she needed until it arrived on a piece of translucent paper. SEX: FEMALE. When my updated birth certificate arrived in the mail, I remember how elated Viv was. She treated me to drinks at a swanky hotel lounge nearby. She held up her cocktail glass, saying, "To you. You won, babe. You absolutely fucking won. Cheers."

Cc

Delia CREASE is a successful children's author. When she visits the Little Blue Bookstore, its owner asks Delia to sign copies of her bestseller *The Man Who Was Unimpressed by Everything*. Later, we see Roy reading to Pauline from it, telling the tale of an apathetic father who takes his curious, excited daughter to a museum. No matter what they encounter, the father counters with "I've seen better." For some reason, the book is narrated by the daughter's shoes, which get increasingly exasperated with him. While watching this scene, Vivian couldn't help wiggling her foot and wanting so badly for the pair of Mary Janes telling the story to kick the apathetic father.

Like the daughter in the children's book, Viv was always ready to be astonished. Truth be told, I thought she over-played her enthusiasm for things. But enthusiasm is conta-gious and a hundred times more useful than indifference. Whenever Viv would date someone new, she would immerse herself in their world. A short, inexhaustive list of things that Viv became briefly obsessed with for guys she dated: soccer, science fiction, glam metal, hiking, and Buddhism. Maybe her openness helps to explain why she liked *Little Blue* so deeply. It tries to cram so much life into ten hours. She had a ten-dency to say yes, to embrace whatever floated into her orbit.

Ren CREASE is a more eccentric character than his wife Delia. He always wears a black T-shirt emblazoned with the phrase LET'S HONKYTONK, he's terribly fond of sarsaparilla soda, and he's terrified of salamanders, which we discover during his spelunking adventure.

The Creases are the first two characters we see on *Little Blue*. We watch them take the ferry to Little Blue Island and pull into the RV Park, where they meet Roy, Pauline, and Visconti. The Creases used to own a bookstore, which they sold to wend their way across North America in their pol-ished silver Airstream.

There are a handful of competing theories explaining why the Creases are on Little Blue Island. The most com-monly held theory is the most logical one: they are travel-ling and decided to visit the island during their travels. Both Viv and I rejected this theory because it's too simple and, yes, too boring. Whatever it may be, *Little Blue* is rarely sim-ple and boring. I leaned towards the theory that the Creases' visit to the island is part of a soda pilgrimage. My evidence is that Ren seems to savour every swig of sarsaparilla soda.

I'm willing to believe he loves the stuff. And if you can spot him drinking anything else on the series, I'll buy you a case of soda.

Viv was convinced the Creases were trying to swindle Roderick Ambleside of a sizeable chunk of his fortune. She had three main pieces of evidence for this theory:

1. Ren was played by Ricky Jay, who was fascinated with con artists and depicted an array of con men in his previous roles. He's also one of the few actors cast before the audition process began, so perhaps *Little Blue*'s creator Jason Bloch had decided before the project started that it would involve a long con. Inside the privacy of the Creases' RV, we do see Ren produce a deck of cards and perform some spectacular sleight-of-hand tricks.
2. He repeatedly mispronounces the word "sarsaparilla." In Viv's eyes this suggested that his interest in this flavour is feigned.
3. We hear a couple of references to the Little Blue Soda Company's top-secret "overcarbonation process," which its competitors seem keen to discover.

Viv and I were both drawn towards Ren's decision to wear the same T-shirt every day. Well, he would wear a fresh shirt, but they all had that same design: a black background with the words LET'S HONKYTONK in large white capital letters across the chest. There's something seductive about people who find a look and commit to it. Viv was a fashion hound and couldn't do it. I tend towards owning multiples of clothing that I like, but I can't bring myself to get multiples that are identical. Sure, I own four flannel shirts of the same brand and design, but each one has a slightly different colour scheme. Meanwhile, Ren owned boxes of identical shirts, which we learn he designed, printed, and failed to sell in the Creases' former bookstore, Our Hospitality Books.

Viv quoted the phrase "Let's honkytonk" from Ren's ubiquitous T-shirt nearly as often as she adapted Tycho's rallying cry of "More soda!" Tycho's line was adaptable to many social situations, whereas Viv used "Let's honkytonk" selectively. Here are a few examples that come to mind:

> › "Let's honkytonk" + jerking her thumb = "Let's leave."
> › "Let's honkytonk" + pointing at an empty glass
>   = "Let's order another drink."
> › "Let's honkytonk" + grabbing her purse in a restaurant
>   = "Let's go to the washroom."

Emma CURWOOD died under mysterious circumstances. Her best friend was Stephanie Marberry.

Emmanuel CURWOOD is Emma's twin brother. Even before we meet Delia and Ren Crease, the series opens with a voice-over of Emmanuel writing a diary entry to his dead sister: *Dear Em, I didn't kill anyone, but people died. The police think I did it.* Emmanuel is a social pariah at Little Blue School because most islanders suspect that he murdered his twin sister, despite evidence to the contrary.

For Mr. Bits's class, he rehearses a scene from *Macbeth* with two classmates, Mitch Marberry and Tracy Kim. He secretly pines for Tracy, who is oblivious to him. Viv, a fashion authority of sorts, thought he would have dramatically increased his chances with her if he lost his floppy hair, turtlenecks, and "aw, shucks" attitude. He also gets flustered and trips over his words when tries to compliment her at the talent show after her stunning performance.

Emmanuel plays Macbeth as timid. Tracy's Lady Macbeth

tramples him in every scene. When she asks Macbeth if he is a man, Emmanuel's Macbeth can't make eye contact with her and quavers, "Ay, and a bold one." His awkwardness is also on display at his part-time job at the bottling plant. He fails to realize that you can only ask so many questions about a co-worker's cup of tea before it becomes annoying. He is the only character seen drinking the Little Blue Soda Company's cucumber soda. It looks like scuzzy pond water.

When you said something amusing, Vivian often laughed just a little too loud. I'll admit that more than a few times I jotted funny things down so I wouldn't forget to tell her about them later. Her appreciative laugh was that delightful. I worked in the gift shop of the art gallery when I met Viv, and I would amuse her with my over-the-top imitations of pretentious customers. I once took her there and gave her a whirlwind tour of iconic works of art turned into tacky souvenirs: Sneakers emblazoned with Andy Warhol electric chairs! Jean-Michel Basquiat SAMO IS DEAD sunglasses! Trucker caps adorned with Frida Kahlo's self-portrait as a wounded deer! Panties with a self-portrait of Emily Carr on the front and a painting of her pet monkey Woo on the back! Viv's unbridled laugh cut through the quiet hum of the gift shop. One of my co-workers shot me a look.

The hardest I ever saw her laugh was when I introduced her to Lil Big Kid, whose raps are written from the point of view of being a toddler. In particular, she lost her mind when I played the song "Juicebox Boy," which contains one of the truly deathless couplets of the twenty-first century:

> *I'm gonna drink juice yes yes and dance*
> *Uh oh! Just made a mess in my big boy pants*

She shrieked the first time she heard that. More than once, I made her wobble with laughter by whispering "just made a mess in my big girl pants" into her ear.

My brother Christopher texted and invited me over for dinner. I needed to get out of the house, so I accepted, knowing our dinner would be something out of a box or a tin can.

Christopher and my parents weren't thrilled about me being trans, but eventually they came around. Since adjusting to that news, Chris has been understanding about plenty of things, but he doesn't get my writing project for Vivian and thinks it was a mistake for me to take a leave of absence from school. Sure, he understands that I was affected by Viv's death, but he doesn't understand why I can't just feel sad for a few days and move on. The upshot is that I knew he wouldn't want to talk about any of the things I've been thinking about lately and that was fine with me because I needed a distraction.

As soon as he let me into his apartment, he opened a bottle of beer and handed it to me. He was making us tuna casserole, according to the open box on the counter. The white glove on the box seemed to be smiling at me.

"To no rain," he said, raising his bottle. He took a swig.

"No rain," I said, taking a sip. The weather is a perennial conversation topic in our drizzly city. I used to tell people that I actually enjoy overcast skies and rain for days, but people just want someone to commiserate with, so I've learned to dial it back.

"I talked to Mom yesterday," he said.

"What did she have to say?" I asked.

"Not much," he said. "She talked a lot about her new washing machine."

"Got it. Anything else?"

"Not really. You should call her."

I shrugged. "I guess. Now that you've told me about the washing machine, I don't know that we'll have much to talk about. How's Annie?"

"I think she's okay. We're not dating anymore. I'm seeing somebody new."

"Oh, that's exciting! What can you tell me? Does she have a name?"

"Alice," he said.

"Alice is a legit name, Chris." I paused. "You can trust an Alice. Alice and Chris. Chris and Alice. It has a certain ring to it."

He finished his beer before putting plates, cutlery, a roll of paper towels, and a bottle of ketchup on the small table. He grabbed a fresh bottle of beer for himself and checked if I needed another one.

I shook my head. "Thanks, though," I said.

His phone started dinging. He turned off the timer and the oven. "And dinner," he said, pausing for dramatic effect, "is served." He carefully set the Dutch oven down on a trivet on the kitchen table and removed the lid.

We ate and chatted about Alice, his job as a stock clerk at Cheaper + Better Foods, and what he'd been watching on TV lately. I didn't bring up Viv or *Little Blue* because I didn't need Chris judging me right then. The tuna casserole wasn't bad, even if it was underseasoned and the noodles were a tad chewy. I sprinkled salt on mine, and Chris covered his in ketchup, as usual.

Chris has always been into comics and can draw anything. When we were growing up, I was incredibly jealous. Okay, I'm still jealous, and I'll always be jealous. If I had any artistic ability, I'd be an artist. Over the years, he's tried to give me pointers, but it comes so naturally to him that he doesn't need to think about it. It's frustrating for both of us. I once spent hours trying repeatedly to draw our cat, Sally. The more I drew her, the worse my drawings seemed to get. Chris took my pencil and in just a few minutes he drew Sally, right down to her thin moustache (or, as we liked to say, "mouse-stache").

After dinner, he showed me a comic he'd started working on. He was going to call it *Stock Clerk!* It was about two stock clerks who were bodybuilders. They were both characterized as being dim-witted and lazy, spending much of their time at work eating bananas and boiled eggs and drinking powdery "muscle shakes." It ended with one of them asking the narrator if he'd ever fantasized about being put in a room with a dog and ripping it apart with his bare hands. When he admitted that he hadn't, the bodybuilding stock clerk just shook his head and walked away.

"These drawings are great, Chris," I said. "But are these based on real people?"

"Yep," he said. "A hundred percent. Those are guys I work with. It's fucked up."

"I agree that it's fucked up," I said. "But I don't think you should publish this. There was some other comic you did about work before that wasn't that bad. I think it had people making ghost noises and eating cookies in the back room. That was harmless. This stuff isn't harmless. Bodybuilders aren't known for their senses of humour."

He tried to change the topic, but I told him I was worried.

"Look, I don't wanna visit you in the hospital," I said. "You changed their names at least, right?"

He shook his head.

"Really, dude? At the very least, you need to change their names or publish it under a pseudonym."

He said he'd think about it, which is often code for "You're right, sis, but I can't admit it just yet."

He left the room and came back with two more bottles of beer. He opened a bag of popcorn and we sat on his mustard-yellow couch to watch some superhero movie. It was full of sound and fury and muscly bros in latex shouting and punching. Towards the end of the film, I started telling Chris that basically every action movie is an indictment of masculinity and how if you removed masculine aggression from the mix, you wouldn't need to combat it with more aggression. He'd heard my schtick before and gave me a look that let me know it was a bummer that his uncool older sister couldn't enjoy action flicks. When his roommate Dirk stumbled in, I drained my beer and gave Chris a quick hug goodbye.

Dd

DIMPLE is a calico cat that lives with Rusty Odell. She spends most of her time sleeping in the lantern room of the lighthouse and appears surprisingly attentive when Rusty reads aloud to her. Whenever Rusty gives Dimple a cat treat, he says "Body of Christ," which is profane and perfect.

Viv would gush when Dimple was onscreen. She loved cats and seldom passed by an outdoor cat that she didn't try to befriend. She certainly loved my cute-as-a-button torty, Whisk.

The density of *Little Blue* still astounds me. It's like a conglomerate rock or a tin of sardines. It shouldn't work and some of the ideas feel like they don't belong, but I'm glad they're there. A prime example is the novel that Rusty reads aloud to Dimple. *Babewolf* is about a baseball-obsessed janitor who, when the moon is full, turns into a werewolf named Babe Lincoln Ruth. Somehow, the wolf wears a baseball uniform and a stovepipe hat while it prowls in the moonlight.

This has to be my favourite passage that Rusty reads to Dimple: "I dreamed about my face being licked by a giraffe with a large gluey tongue. I awoke, groggy and exhausted, dressed in a torn vintage Red Sox uniform caked with blood."

Jason Bloch has famously (and repeatedly) claimed that he literally stumbled into filmmaking when he tripped on a crudely made papier-mâché figure on the set of a student film. At the time, he was becoming increasingly disillusioned with his studies in printmaking and offered to create stylized paper figures for a stop-motion sequence in the low-budget film. His background in art history and printmaking is evident in his first experimental short film, *Saint Juniper*, which merged shots of intricate Victorian-era design patterns with hand-tinted found footage of lumberjacks felling trees. It's a tedious exercise in style.

The seed for Bloch's ambitious first feature film, *The James Gang*, was planted when he realized that infamous outlaws Frank and Jesse James were contemporaries of celebrated writers William and Henry James. Bloch worked for months with his four main actors to develop their characters independently, a technique he would incorporate into his later projects. Meanwhile, Bloch also helped dozens of other actors to create the wives, lovers, friends, rivals, enemies, victims, bartenders, sheriffs, editors, publishers, and sundry other characters the four James brothers would meet. After the extensive exploration period, it took a mere four months to improvise and film *The James Gang*. Unfortunately, it took nearly a year to edit these scenes into a (mostly) coherent film.

The James Gang surprised audiences with its unusual pacing (alternating between languid and frenetic), its electronic music soundtrack (comprising unearthed Kraftwerk outtakes), its unique hand-tinted sequences (reminiscent of the ones in *Saint Juniper*), and its literary dialogue (much of it quoting or paraphrasing the writings of William and Henry James). As soon as it premiered at the Toronto International Film Festival, *The James Gang* was lauded by critics. Roger Ebert's oft-quoted review characterized it as "one great blooming, buzzing masterpiece."

It's a unique and confusing epic that probably deserves both its acclaim and its criticism. But it has an emotional heft that few films can rival. For example, the scene where Henry James (played by Jim Broadbent at his most vulnerable) hires a sex worker and is unable to get an erection is devastating. After she leaves the room with money in hand, Henry slowly curls in the fetal position and murmurs, "Jesse, my sweet, sweet Jesse." It doesn't help that the camera lingers on Henry murmuring and cradling his knees for a full sixty seconds as it pulls back to show a wide angle of the room. We can't help seeing Henry as something small and trembling beside the bed.

The year after *The James Gang* was released, Jason Bloch was awarded a MacArthur Fellowship "genius grant" that included a no-strings-attached cash prize of $500,000. Before long, he announced that he had agreed to develop a television series for a new network, Fine Media.

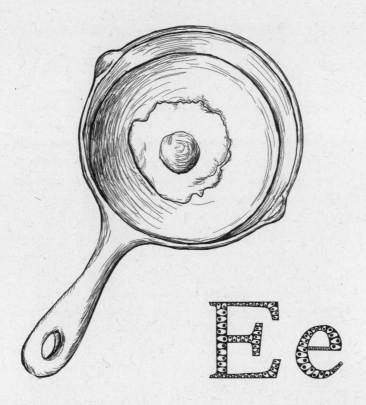

Ivy ELDER was Roy Spittle's wife and Pauline Elder's mother. Ivy died in a boating accident along with her parents. She was an architect who worked on several projects on the island, most notably Tycho Brahe's castle and observatory, which she completed shortly before her death.

It probably has nothing to do with Ivy Elder, but there is a song called "Ivy" on Frank Ocean's album *Blonde*. It isn't about death or architecture. It's a celebration of vulnerability. Before hearing the song, I wouldn't have imagined the phrase "armored truck " could make me teary. But it does.

If you could see my thoughts, you would see our faces
Safe in my rental like an armored truck back then
We didn't give a fuck back then

I'm moved by the security Frank felt with his lover. Viv gave me that. I felt protected. Being around her gave me confidence. I saw a way forward, a way of being trans in the world that didn't seem like a struggle. We were opposites in so many ways. She was thin; I'm not. She was straight; I'm not. She was a vegetarian; I'm not. She was outgoing; I'm not. But she took me under her wing. If she hadn't, I'm not sure what would have happened. She softened my shame and anxiety about being trans. She showed me that it was possible to wade through that river and reach the other side. Since Viv's death, sometimes I play a song like "Ivy" that hits me in the sternum to coax the first few tears and, once there's a leak, this dyke can't hold back the water. Somehow crying helps me feel okay in the world. It allows me to channel my feelings, to cleanse myself. Before I started taking femme pills, I barely cried. Now I rarely go a week without weeping.

Listening to "Ivy" now, I'm reminded that a few days before releasing his first major label album, Frank Ocean astonished everyone by publishing an open-hearted letter online that revealed his first love was another man. His love was unrequited, but Frank said he stayed friends with his first love because he couldn't imagine a life without him. Then he writes, "I don't have any secrets I need kept anymore." He says he's grateful to his first love for what they had, even though it wasn't what he imagined and wasn't enough. Still, he's thankful. I try to practice that kind of gratitude, but it's hard.

Pauline ELDER is the daughter of Roy Spittle and Ivy Elder. Pauline's favourite things in the world seem to be her dad, her dog, and her best friend, Tristan Jha.

Pauline's favourite children's book is called *One, Two, It's Wonderful to Meet You*. We see Roy read it to her before bed twice. It's a brightly illustrated counting book that was one of the last gifts Pauline received from her grandparents, Paul and Marjorie Elder. Each time Roy reads the book to her, he talks about her mom and how much she loved Pauline.

Then he reads the inscription on the book's flyleaf:

Dearest Pauline, We're counting on getting to know you better and better. We can't wait to see you again!

All our love,
Gran and Gramps
xoxo

Carter EXBY drives a forklift at the Little Blue Soda Company's warehouse. He seems to spend much of his free time sipping milky tea and looking out the window of his small apartment, which faces the lighthouse.

Carter prints a newsletter on his own mimeograph machine. We only see the *Carter Exby Bulletin* onscreen for a few seconds. Blink and it glides by you. If you pause the episode and study the front page of the *Carter Exby Bulletin*, you get a different picture of Carter's world. You learn that he belongs to a local knitting circle, plays trumpet in his own "smoky jazz quartet" called the Carter Quartexby, and has been rehearsing to perform the role of Helmsworthy, a narcoleptic butler, in the musical *Ain't Too Proud to Sleep*. This depiction of Carter Exby differs from the sedate character we see. Clearly, he has an active social life that is not depicted on *Little Blue*, or he has an active imagination. Intriguingly, we never learn why (and for whom) Carter publishes this newsletter.

Vivian enjoyed *Little Blue* when she first watched it, but she really fell for the series when she stumbled on a copy of Lucy Six's *Carter Exby Bulletin*. Lucy's zine showed how deep the *Little Blue* rabbit hole goes and how many Easter eggs it has. She seemed to have watched every episode frame by frame in her hunt for elusive Easter eggs. Carter's bulletin was the first egg Viv showed me, and I was astounded that so much energy had been put into creating an alternate existence for this character that was compressed into three seconds of screen time, which only the show's most zealous fans might see. Suddenly, the character of Carter Exby was no longer a timid forklift driver; he was enigmatic and, like nearly every character on the series, harboured a secret life.

Among Viv's small collection of books were her copies of the zine *Carter Exby Bulletin*. So many of the observations about *Little Blue* that I've scattered throughout this book were gleaned from Lucy Six's indispensable zine. (You should subscribe to her zine and send her your money.[2] Seriously, she's amazing.) I would be remiss if I didn't also acknowledge how valuable I have found Claire Kubo and Jay Ryu's *Little Blue*–dedicated website, The Little Blue Soda Company. (A thousand thank yous to Lucy, Claire, Jay, and many other *Little Blue* devotees who have written obsessively about the show.)

---

2   To get your hands on her mail-order-only zine send your cash to Lucy Six at this address:
Amstel 218
1017 AJ
Amsterdam
The Netherlands

I'm hesitant to talk about Viv's secret life, but she didn't really have one; she was open about who she was with anyone who knew her. Part of my hesitation is that she's dead and she did a lot of things that could be seen as sordid. But she refused to be ashamed or apologetic, which I respected. After we'd known each other for a while, she started alluding to things she had done or was planning to do. Some of these things sounded horrifying to me and I was sure she was kidding. She wasn't and revealed a few examples of bodily evidence, one being a sizeable scar on her upper back of an ankh. It had been carved into her with a straight razor. My face must have contorted because she told me she was fine, that she loved this scar. After that, we didn't talk much about her ongoing dalliance with excess. She would casually touch on things, but she knew that I wasn't keen on hearing details. I'd occasionally notice bruises blooming on her thighs, and she assured me that they were consensual, that she enjoyed displaying these tender mementos.

I didn't think Viv was religious, but after her death a few of her friends told me she identified as a Blakean. When I asked what that meant, one of them pointed me to a Wikipedia page. Apparently, Blakeans follow the writings of William Blake and "embrace experience, exuberance, and excess." I'm all for experience and exuberance, but the idea of excess scares me. Viv claimed that she could experience deeper beauty and learn more about herself and the world by throwing her arms around excess. Maybe that's true, but I'm squeamish when it comes to testing and expanding my body's limits. And I was worried she would get hurt or worse when engaging in new things, especially with people she didn't know that well. But she trusted her judgement even when it was impaired. I know on at least one occasion her choices took her to a place beyond where she was prepared to go. I didn't find out about this experience until after her death, but the friend who told me about it also said that Viv had worked through it and stopped putting herself in situations where anything similar was likely to happen.

In one of Viv's boxes in my closet, I discovered a hefty book of William Blake's poetry and prose that must have weighed five pounds. The first fifty or so pages were riddled with underlining, highlighting, marginalia, and sticky notes. The next 900-plus pages were relatively clean. Viv never talked to me about Blake. When I read his work, I could immediately see why she'd been drawn to him. So many of his lines seemed like they could have come out of Viv's mouth. On second thought, I was pretty sure I'd heard her say a few of his lines, including "exuberance is beauty" and "energy is eternal delight." Ah, Viv. You rascally, charming plagiarist.

In the same box as the Blake book were a dozen or so novels, a handful of biographies, and a few self-help books I hadn't noticed when I was packing the box. The only self-help book with tangible proof that Viv had read it was one called *Happy! Happy!! Happy!!!* by Dr. Brett Gray, PhD. The chapter of the book Viv had earmarked and annotated was called "Feeling Alphabetter." It describes a "self-talk technique" for using the "ABCs of me" to feel good about yourself. To illustrate this idea Dr. Gray runs through the alphabet, listing things he could remind himself of throughout the day: "I am Ambitious! I am Brave! I am Capable! I am Dependable!" and so on. When he gets to the end of the alphabet ("I am Youthful! I am Zesty!"), he loops back to the beginning to hammer the point home. "I am Affectionate! I am Bright! I am Creative! I am Diligent!" and on and on. The chapter is quite brief and playful, as when Dr. Gray writes, "Remember: Don't say your self-talk out loud. Say it in your mind with your invisible lips." I wondered if Viv had actually tried the feeling alphabetter technique and I suspected she had because she'd jotted down a list of positive alphabetical adjectives in the margin: *adorable*, *bold*, *cute*, *delightful*, *energetic*, etc. All of them applied to her, and I felt a twinge of sadness knowing that Viv needed to remind herself of her good qualities. But I knew that Viv's self-confidence wasn't innate, that she'd had to work at it, that she probably had to work to regain it every time her heart was crumpled by some handsome disappointment or another.

To a certain extent, *Little Blue* owes its existence to flamboyant tycoon Stanley Fine's inferiority complex. He created Fine Media primarily as an attempt to build a legacy that would rival that of his father, Mort Fine, who founded Fine Computers. Shortly after Mort Fine died, his son swiftly sold his pioneering technology company to create his own HBO-style subscription network, which he saw as the perfect vehicle for his wealth and creative energy. He infamously promised his fledgling Fine Media network would include three original "genius-level" television series, which were being created by Zero Astor, David Cronenberg, and Jason Bloch.

Zero Astor helmed several acclaimed idiosyncratic documentaries before developing a series for Fine Media, *Tabitha Starling*, which would be his first work of fiction. It would be co-written by his daughter, Zada, who would also be its star. *Tabitha Starling* is about a beautiful dog walker who solves crimes in New York City during the early seventies. Gilbert Gottfried signed on to play the title character's father, Jim Starling, a hapless meteorologist. Apparently, Zero Astor repeatedly told Gottfried that he should "make it a smidge more Seinfeld" while pretending to twist a small imaginary volume knob on a machine that Gottfried came to call the Seinfeld-o-meter. Gottfried had no interest in pretending to be Jerry Seinfeld. Between takes, Gottfried would occasionally do his devastating Seinfeld impression to amuse the crew and annoy Astor. I could only watch the first couple episodes of the series. An anonymous online reviewer described watching the show as "uncomfortable in the way it would be uncomfortable being around a Great Dane with diarrhea" and they weren't wrong.

Donzerly Light, David Cronenberg's series for Fine Media, was going to be about an entomologist who discovers an iridescent insect species that rapidly decimates the world's population. The deadly species is named *Cotinis donzerlylighti* as an ode to the entomologist's estranged daughter, who had once asked him what "donzerly light" was. The series began to unravel when John C Reilly, who was set to play the entomologist, broke his ankle in a freak dune-buggy accident the day before filming was to begin. Rather than wait for Reilly to heal or recast the lead role, Cronenberg, who detested Stanley Fine constantly describing *Donzerly Light* to the media as "beyond genius level," pulled the plug on the series, citing creative differences with the network.

Jason Bloch has described *Little Blue* as beginning with the "fuzzy notion" that it would be set on a tiny island. Part of his rationale was that he wanted to explore the idea that "things evolve strangely in isolation. Look at the Galapagos. When you are cut off from the rest of the world, you develop differently. Your snout might begin to curve. Your wings might get brighter. That's how I began to see the characters on this little dot of an island. They were kind of like bugs that blew across the ocean, landed in a strange new environment and started slowly adapting." The audition process for the show lasted a few months and spanned North America. If actors intrigued Bloch during an audition, he would cast them on the spot. He did not have characters for them in mind, but knew that he would be able to work with them individually to build characters from scratch that would populate the island.

After the casting process, Bloch decamped to develop the series on Cruikshank Island in British Columbia. Within days, dozens of actors and crew members arrived on the island. As he had done earlier during preparations for *The James Gang*, Bloch was careful to keep the actors separated—not an easy task on an island that is twenty-six square kilometres and has a population of 850 (not including the *Little Blue* cast and crew). Aside from one minor incident, the actors seem to have kept to themselves during the months of one-to-one character-building exercises with Bloch, who was spread very thin between all of his actors. He later admitted that he only slept a few hours a night while floating between trailers parked in far-flung spots around the island to conduct intense consultations with all of the actors.

After the extensive preparation process, Bloch jotted down a list of the scenes that would form the backbone for *Little Blue*. He did not know what any of the dialogue would be or what shape the scenes would take. For example, the voice-overs at the start of each episode stem from Bloch's terse note, "Emmanuel writes in diary." Through improvising and refining the journal entries, Bloch and actor Archie Braemore (playing Emmanuel) determined how Emmanuel's sister Emma had died , as well as the content of each journal entry to her. Bloch used this process for every character and every scene. He would then allow for a certain amount of improvisation and ideas from the cast and crew so he would have options during post-production.

Immediately after filming wrapped, Bloch and editor Tina Veverka, who had painstakingly assembled *The James Gang*, began sifting through hundreds of hours of footage. Stanley Fine was delighted to hear that Bloch was happy with what he was seeing in the editing room. Several months later, Fine was aggravated that not a single episode had been corralled into a rough cut yet. He had promised subscribers that three new series would air soon and now that number had already been whittled to two: *Tabitha Starling* and *Little Blue*.

When *Little Blue* finally aired, it flew under the radar of most critics and viewers. The few critics who deigned to write about the series were either underwhelmed or baffled. A representative piece painted it as "a show that has characters so wacky and unbelievable that they make the Log Lady [on *Twin Peaks*] look like Carol Brady [on *The Brady Bunch*]." The review concluded by taking Stanley Fine's network to task: "Why would any viewer pony up to subscribe to this 'premium channel' when it has only produced two shows—and they're both worse than the queer but demure *I Love Lucy* reboot, *Ethel Loves Lucy*? Fine Media, you got some 'splainin' to do." Indeed, Stanley Fine was harangued by his network's subscribers; they were infuriated to be paying $8.99 a month for a specialty channel that consisted largely of *M*A*S*H* reruns.

A few days after *Little Blue*'s final episode aired, Fine Media quietly announced that it was "suspending operations until further notice." A month later, the operation folded entirely and Stanley Fine was onto his next project, a short-lived email service called Finemail.

Ff

Dalton FLUDD is a quiet tugboat driver who seems to spend most of his time writing poetry. There are several shots of him scribbling in a small blue notebook on the deck of his tugboat. The only writing of Dalton's the viewers glimpse is a rough draft of a poem called "Plum Black Coffee." The page is covered with strikethroughs and water-smudged doodles. Only the poem's final two lines are legible:

> *Drifting among the fixed stars*
> *Thinking only of sleep.*

His best friend is Roy Spittle.

Dalton is also remembered as the character who trips near Chappy Park on an unexploded bomb, which turns out to be a harmless prop from a low-budget comedy that was filmed on Little Blue Island in the sixties.

I've been cagey about this writing project. It's hard to know how to even mention it without sounding bonkers. "I'm writing an encyclopedia about a television show for a friend of mine who died." So far, I've only told three people who I trust. Dot, Christopher, and Lila. Lila is an artist friend of mine who works on a mess of different projects at once, all of which bring in just enough money to keep her afloat. When Lila was over one day, she started flipping through Viv's *Squid Encyclopedia for Kids* while I was making coffee in the kitchen.

When I came back with a carafe of coffee and a couple of mugs, she was absorbed in the encyclopedia.

"Do you need anything for your coffee? Honey? Cream? Milk?" I asked.

"Black's great," she said.

I put a mug on the coffee table in front of her.

"Thanks. The illustrations in this book are gorgeous. Do you think I could borrow it?"

That's when I explained what I'd been doing for the past few months and the role of the encyclopedia.

She'd met Vivian a couple of times. They weren't fast friends. Viv thought Lila was pretentious, and Lila thought Viv was uncouth. One vivid memory that encapsulates their oil-and-vinegar relationship happened the last time we hung out together. We made small talk in a coffee shop while Lila drew our three faces on a napkin. We probably talked about the weather, dating, mutual friends, work, rent, the usual.

When Lila finished her drawing, she used the napkin to wipe the watery counter under her iced coffee. Viv said she had to go and left after a couple of quick hugs.

That night, she sent me a string of sour text messages about Lila.

sorry but i don't like your friend
why did she have to keep saying ladies
yes we ARE fucking ladies
that drawing of me was the worst
are you fucking her
sorry
hope you had a good night babe
hugs
<3

Viv's message reminded me that a couple of times Lila had imitated our barista, who welcomed us by asking, "What can I get for you lay-dees," really emphasizing the last word, probably to signify that, yes, she noticed two of us were trans and she was trying to be affirming in a "go trans girl, go" kinda way. Viv and I were used to it, but Lila probably hadn't experienced it before, so she thought it was funny. The next day, I messaged Lila to fill her in on the "lay-dees" situation.

When I told Lila about the encyclopedia project for Viv, she offered to make some drawings for it. She suggested having a single illustration per letter. As soon as she said it, I knew she was right. Twenty-six drawings sounded perfect.

"But I thought you didn't like Viv," I said.

"Oh, I liked Vivian," she said. "But I could tell she didn't like me. And I didn't want to force a friendship. I get it if someone doesn't wanna be friends with me. Half the time I don't wanna be friends with me." She laughed. "I really wanted her to like me because you two were so close."

"It's my fault. I'm not good at the whole social thing."

"I'm not good at social stuff either," she said. "When I don't clam up entirely, I ask a silly question like 'Where are you from?' They tell me and I say something like 'Oh, cool' and check my phone or start doodling on a scrap of paper."

"Yeah, you do spend a lot of time doodling in public."

She was drawing tiny cats on the cover of a free weekly newspaper on my coffee table. She stopped drawing for a sec. "Guilty as charged. But it's better at calming me down than any meds."

The next day, Lila messaged me to reiterate that she would be happy to draw images for the encyclopedia. Despite her comments about the napkin portraits, I knew Viv had appreciated Lila's art. She'd even coveted a silkscreened tote of mine covered in small drawings by Lila. A toothbrush. A tube of lipstick. A sleeping cat. A pencil. A houseplant. A lemon. Viv had wanted to get a similar tote but Lila had stopped making them. The only bag still in stock was the same one that I already had. Viv thought it would be tacky if we ever hung out and had the same bag. I told her we'd just look like twins, but she wasn't into it. Part of the reason I'd introduced Viv to Lila was so she could ask her directly about silkscreening more tote bags. Viv could be quite persuasive when she wanted to be. But they barely talked. Viv kept texting someone and didn't mention tote bags at all. Lila settled into drawing a tree with a bike rack under it. I tried to steer them into a conversation but neither of them seemed keen to chat. After a while, I grew quieter and nibbled on my jumbo cinnamon bun. I occupied myself with trying to wipe its sticky goo off my hands between bites. I'd occasionally punctuate the silence by pointing out a cute dog walking by the window or by offering them some of my bun. Even with that strained initial meeting, I thought they would get along better if we all met again. I was wrong.

For the encyclopedia drawings, I sent Lila an alphabetical list of objects related to Viv or *Little Blue*. Some letters were really difficult. When in doubt, I asked her to draw an animal. It's hard to go wrong with animal illustrations. The first drawing she made was of an armadillo. As soon as I saw it, I knew the illustrations were going to work. I'm particularly fond of the "fuck you" gesture at the start of this section. (*F Is for Fuck You* sounds like the title of a young adult book parents are forever trying to ban from public libraries.) Out of the blue, Lila also started sending me hand-drawn upper-case and lower-case letters to accompany each illustration.

If you go to Lila's website, you can see more of her work, including silkscreened prints, T-shirts, and tote bags. You can also see a drawing of herself at the bottom of the "About Me" section that was inspired by the cover of Viv's *Squid Encyclopedia for Kids*. Lila's colourful illustration portrays her as an adorable, artistic octopus, each of her arms doing something creative—painting, drawing, pecking at a laptop, brandishing a silkscreening squeegee, etc.

Grady GOODWIN runs the island's drive-in movie the-atre. It's revealed that he was a famous musician in the sixties, though the only character who seems to know about his past life is Agnes Pennypacker, who accidentally calls him Bobby while they're taking her dog for a walk. Before changing his name and retreating to Little Blue Island, he was known as Bobby Blinkhorn and was best-known as a member of the Snickersnee, a band from Indianapolis that was mistakenly seen as part of the British Invasion and whose fame flared and faded with their lone hit, "I Choose You (To Be My Girl)."

Viv lamented that there were no drive-ins near us like the one Grady runs. She could watch black-and-white films all day and sometimes did. I tried joining her once, but the films were too slow and the acting was too stilted for me. During quiet moments, I made a few amusing comments about what was happening onscreen. Viv wasn't amused. She never talked during films. Ever. If you went to the theatre with her, you'd most likely witness (or be on the receiving end of) her well-honed "shush" ability. She would have made a great librarian.

One time Viv and I were talking about fictional hit songs written for films and TV shows that are actually catchy. Viv refused to acknowledge that the Snickersnee's "I Choose You (To Be My Girl)" from *Little Blue* is a bona fide earworm. I'll grant that the song is nutty. After all, the chorus revolves around a fake sneeze and a hackneyed rhyme: "Ah-ah-ah-CHOOse you to be my girl. You know ah-CHOOse you to rule my world." The next couple of lines are even worse: "I lose control when I sneeze. I'm beggin' please, please, please." Then, the music stops for a couple of seconds before we hear the languid a capella line: "Don't be so … cold." And, suddenly, after the delicate, unhurried harmony vocals on those four words, the music surges in and starts dipping and swerving like a wobbly top that finally stops spinning when the song ends.

Vivian hated the song. She thought it served as an on-the-nose period detail of how horrible sixties music was. Then again, she didn't enjoy most music recorded before the eighties. To her ears, it sounded dusty and dirty. Britpop was her wheelhouse. She called it the "perfect trans girl soundtrack." She was even known to claim that the Beatles were "not bad," but they were no Suede. Whenever I'd bring up the Beatles, Viv would cut me off with five words: "Beep

beep, beep beep, yeah." I would stammer something about her love of old black-and-white horror films, but she would wave off my criticism. "Totally different," she said. End of discussion. Grrrrr.

In the early days of our friendship, Viv made me a playlist called *My Life in 16 Songs*:

1. Suede - "Beautiful Ones"
2. Pulp - "Mis-Shapes"
3. The Present Tints - "Baby Gamma"
4. Elastica - "Vaseline"
5. Primal Scream - "Velocity Girl"
6. Sometimes the Sun - "Slippery Like a Fox"
7. Sleeper - "Swallow"
8. Oasis - "Whatever" (radio edit version)
9. PJ Harvey - "Dress"
10. Lush - "Ciao!" (ft. Jarvis Cocker)
11. Blur - "Girls and Boys"
12. The Boo Radleys - "Wish I Was Skinny"
13. Costumes by Edith Head - "Essex"
14. The Smiths - "Half a Person"
15. Portishead - "Glory Box"
16. Suede – "Stay Together"

She'd drawn a heart around the "16" on the playlist she gave me. I soon learned that she tended to attach hearts to things, whether it was something she'd written by hand or something she'd typed on her phone. If you knew Viv, you'd see more <3s in one day than seemed possible. She also had a tendency to verbalize her feelings by saying things like "sigh" or "blink" or "purr" or "swoon."

I thought it was charming that she'd made me a mix of her personal soundtrack. Britpop wasn't my style, but it gave me a better sense of how she saw herself and I started to appreciate how Suede could be more important to her than the Beatles.

Even though the verses to a song like "Beautiful Ones" were shallow, the chorus had a vitality and grandeur that reminded me of her femme swagger . She tended to listen to music while walking and moved with purpose. I can imagine "Beautiful Ones" blaring as Viv strides through the streets with a thousand other trans women.

> *Oh, here they come*
> *The beautiful ones*
> *The beautiful ones*
> *La la la la*

When Viv introduced me to *Little Blue*, I just assumed she'd been turned on to the series through dating some handsome guy who was a fan. But, no, it was Suede. She got into the show because Suede's song "Sleeping Pills" opened the fifth episode. Viv's love for Suede was intense. The first time I visited her apartment, she'd made me cocktails and introduced me to her favourite band.

When I first listened to *My Life in 16 Songs*, I recognized how most of these tracks would have resonated with Viv. But I didn't understand how important they'd been to her sense of self until I watched her perform "Mis-Shapes" at karaoke.

> *We'd like to go to town but we can't risk it, oh*
> *'Cause they just want to keep us out*
> *You could end up with a smack in the mouth*
> *Just for standing out, now, really*

Apparently, this song was written for people who feel like

outcasts. After seeing Viv sing it, I can't hear it as anything other than a song about being trans. The threat of being seen in public, being excluded, and being attacked are all much more acute for trans folks (especially trans women of colour) than for your typical my-peers-just-don't-understand-me outcasts.

Viv was always willing to risk going to town and unwilling to be kept out. By comparison, my life was quite small. I didn't go out much. I didn't travel. It took me quite a while to feel comfortable with the weight of additional eyes on me. At first, it made me self-conscious. I was thrown by people's reactions. Is that person confused by me? Is that guy embarrassed for me? Why did that person just swivel their head to watch me cross the street?

Viv expanded my orbit. She helped me to be trans in the world. She didn't school me on any reductive rules of femininity. She just let me see how she was able to be strong and femme and trans and stay alive.

She also said early on that I could ask her anything . I've always been shy and never want to cross any lines. I'm the sort of person who will get cozy in the bathtub and never want to get out. Even making friends has always seemed like magic when I've seen it happen or it's happened to me. But it's never felt like a magic that I have any control over. When I try to make it happen, I always do the wrong thing or say the wrong thing. So, I didn't want to ask Viv the wrong question, even though she'd said all questions were acceptable.

After a few too many drinks one night, I finally asked her via text message how she remained so confident and unflappable. I sent the text and immediately regretted it, but I couldn't take it back, so I just had another glass or two of Malbec, brushed my teeth, and went to bed.

The next morning, I saw she'd replied with a cascade of texts:

oh that
it's gold dust + glitter
it's a perfume i call Defiant Beauty
it smells like FUCK YOU, I AM PRETTY
i dab it on before i go out
it's yours if you want it
let's pancake for breakfast, ok?

I wish I could say that I've gotten to a place where I can dab
a little Defiant Beauty on me before I go out, but the truth
is that I'm still far too self-conscious. Around Viv I felt more
calm and confident than I've ever felt on my own. Small talk
stresses me out terribly. I wish I could calm my mind, but
no matter how much I meditate it doesn't seem to translate
into making it easier to navigate the real world. One technique I sometimes use to calm myself down is to remember
that everyone around me will be dead in a hundred years.
So, eventually, no one will remember the time I accidentally
bumped into that older woman behind me in the super-
market and apologized and she looked at me with complete
contempt and I suddenly felt so uncomfortable and crummy
and delicate that I had to put down my shopping basket and
rush home to curl up in my bed with Whisk. Sure, it's mor-
bid to remind yourself that everyone around you will die,
but at times that reminder feels comforting and necessary.
The stakes are suddenly lower. Sometimes just walking into a
restaurant by myself and sitting down can feel terrifying.

Clara GORSE was one of Viv's least favourite characters.
Clara's humourlessness, religiosity, and prudishness touched
a nerve. Unlike me, she wasn't taken in by her homesteader
stylishness. (Really, Viv? What's not to love about a woman
in a gingham dress and bonnet travelling to town daily in a
horse and buggy who cusses with phrases like "Fudge on a

cracker!'"?) Viv had no patience for parents who didn't want their kids to grow up.

Freddy GORSE's bullying of Tristan Jha is excused by some fans as stemming from the powerlessness he experiences around his domineering mother, Clara. Trickle-down bullying. Really, the kid just seems like a racist jerk. Everything he does seems to sprout from a seed of meanness in him. Look at his ventriloquy at the talent show. His dummy Whompy insults the judges, the audience, and the other talent show contestants.

> WHOMPY: These kids should just give up. They suck. I rule.
> FREDDY: Uh, c'mon, Whompy, some of them are talented.
> *Whompy rolls his eyes.*
> WHOMPY: Who are the sourpusses at that table?
> FREDDY: Those are the judges, Whompy.
> WHOMPY: *They* are judging *me*?! They look like clowns. Clowns with sticks in their buttholes.
> FREDDY: You're embarrassing me, Whompy. Be nice to them. One of them is my teacher.
> WHOMPY: Oh, really? Is it that loser? Cheer up, baby. Whompy loves you.

The funniest part of that talent show sequence is when Whompy tries repeatedly to get the audience, who he's just insulted, to chant his name. "Whompy! Whompy! Whompy! C'mon, chant for me, dummies!" Vivian didn't like Freddy, but she couldn't get enough of Whompy.

Melanie GORSE, Clara's oldest daughter, rebels against her religious upbringing by dating Mitch Marberry, a second-rate rockabilly dude in a leather jacket who drives a muscle car. When Clara finds Melanie holding hands with Mitch, she overreacts by slapping him and dragging away her mortified daughter. Melanie only seems to let her emotions out when she is in the safety of the stables with her horse, Inky.

Roland GORSE farms a plot of land with his wife, Clara. He secretly gambles on pigeon racing and seems to aspire to be a stand-up comedian. If so, the routine he practices in front of goats and sheep is tragically unfunny. Nobody wants to hear that many jokes about poop.

When Melanie, Roland, and Freddy suddenly begin losing their vocabularies, Clara attaches spiritual significance to being "spared" by God. Okay, scratch what I said about her homespun stylishness. To decide that your wicked family has been cursed for their sins and you have been blessed for your piousness is unforgivable.

The cause of the Gorses' sudden loss of language has been vigorously debated by fans. Viv thought the most plausible theory was the simplest one: Freddy, Melanie, and Roland visited a family friend on White Peach Island shortly before their vocabularies started deteriorating. She felt they'd picked up a virus or a parasite from someone on White Peach, which is the same theory Lucy Six floats in an early issue of *Carter Exby Bulletin*. I have no theory. All I know is the first time I watched the Gorses' unexpected loss of language was harrowing. Initially, it's cute. Freddy calls a spoon a "scoopy." Melanie calls a hamburger a "cow sandwich." Roland refers to raindrops as "water pebbles." Then, in the final episode, we watch aghast as their grasp on language unravels entirely and all three of them are left unable to speak, unable to write, and unable to read.

No matter how many times I watch the series, my heart cracks like crème brûlée during the scene where Roland tries repeatedly to communicate through Whompy after he loses his knowledge of language. Roland finally collapses and sobs violently. (No, I can't explain how Whompy embraces Roland and wipes away his tears with a bandana, but I do appreciate that he rolls his eyes while comforting Roland. Always the insult dummy, even when he's showing that he has a heart.)

I find Melanie's final words before entirely losing language deeply satisfying, possibly because of her fraught relationship with her mom. Her final words are revealing and bodily; they twist the emotional knife. Bump. Dump. Hump. Pump. Rump. And her unexpected final word before she loses language entirely: Stump. It's a puzzling word that rhymes with the others but doesn't really fit with them tonally. Stump. Vivian was disappointed by this final word, but I think it shows Melanie refusing to reveal her final thoughts to her mom, kind of like Iago at the end of *Othello*. Melanie says the word so many times that it loses meaning, and then she continues saying it, long after her brother and dad have lost language entirely. She also acts as though everyone should understand her, even though she is saying one word again and again and again. Roland and Freddy are clearly distressed by their deteriorating vocabularies, while Melanie seems to enjoy clanging the same word repeatedly, almost pushing its dull sound towards meaning. Insisting on the stumpness of this stumpy life. I think it's a final act of linguistic rebellion to intentionally bewilder her mom. It works beautifully.

Stump stump, stump stump stump stump stump stump stump stump stump stump. Stump stump stump stump stump stump stump stump stump.

Stump stump stump stump stump, stump stump stump stump stump stump stump stump. Stump. Stump? Stump stump. Stump. **"**

Even though Viv wasn't fond of Clara, she found it difficult to resist occasionally adopting her authoritative use of first-person plural. "We must take our face out of our hands and look at our mother." "We know holding hands seems safe, but it's a quaint town we pass through just before reaching Penetrationville." Part of the seductiveness of Clara's use of "we" and "our" is that she implicates the audience when she makes a statement we might disagree with, such as "Our lives would be much improved if we remembered that self-control is always more powerful than birth control." Oh, Clara.

Vivian once convinced me to watch two episodes of *Danger Bay* with her. She promised that I could be little spoon while we watched. If you haven't seen *Danger Bay*, it's very eighties, very Canadian, and very low budget. It's about a family that lives at an aquarium and solves mysteries involving marine animals and nefarious yachtsmen. For the first while, I just enjoyed being spooned, half watching this goofy half-baked show. Then, suddenly, there was Janet Burkholder, the actress who would go on to play Clara Gorse on *Little Blue*. She looked stunning in her wetsuit, playing a plucky scuba diver named Lazaria. I gazed up at Viv and squeezed her arm. She smiled. "I thought you'd like this," she said, kissing the crown of my head. While she cradled me on the couch, we watched young floppy-haired dweeb Jonah develop a two-episode-long crush on her. (Spoiler alert: His heart gets bruised when he learns that she is the underwater arsonist. He asks, "But why did you do it, Lazaria?" She shrugs, and says, "Just to watch it burn." Thunk. She lances him like a boil. His hangdog expression is priceless.)

Viv found my appetite for cuddling adorable. I'm a cuddle slut. Period. I would have gladly watched four hours of *Danger Bay* as her little spoon. I would even be willing to take turns being little spoon and big spoon. She could only take cuddling in small doses. If a guy wanted to cuddle after they'd fucked, she'd let him, but it wasn't her thing. It's too bad because she could fold me in her arms better than nearly anyone.

One drunken night she surprised me by asking if I could spoon her. Yes. The answer to that question was always going to be yes. After a few minutes, she whispered, "I might have the cleanest asshole on the planet." I was puzzled, but I just hugged her and said something noncommittal like "ah" or "uh-huh." At the time, I didn't really want to know any details. After she died, I happened to mention this to a mutual friend. It turns out she was legendarily into being rimmed by the guys she dated. If a guy wanted her to suck his cock, he had to tongue her asshole first. The thought of these bros lapping at her little asshole brought me so much joy. It sounds like you probably did have one of the cleanest assholes ever, Viv.

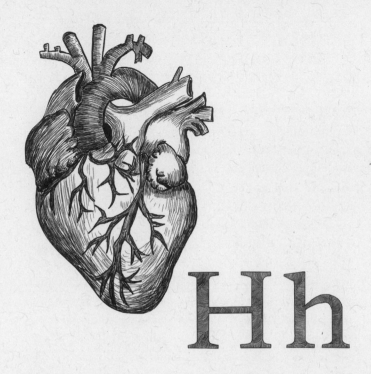

Derek HANDS is the dishwasher at Little Blue Diner. He is good friends with Timmy Whiffle and drinks an obscene amount of caffeine, which worries the members of the Kim family, who own the diner.

" OLIVER: How many cups of coffee do you drink a day?
DEREK: It depends how thirsty I am.
OLIVER: I'm worried about you, Mr. Hands. You need to be careful or you'll have a heart attack by the time you're forty.

DEREK: Don't worry. It's good for what ails me.

OLIVER: What ails you so much that you need to make yourself shake like a tectonic plate?

DEREK: I'm fine. Sometimes I get wobbly. That's life. **99**

While writing about *Little Blue* and Viv, I was contacted unexpectedly by Eric Minor, the actor who played Derek Hands. Eric was trying to write a book about his life as a working actor and the project kept stalling. For some reason, he'd reached out to Claire and Jay who helm the *Little Blue* fan site the Little Blue Soda Company. They had other commitments and suggested he contact me, likely because I happen to live in the same city as Eric. As I was on hiatus from grad school and broke, I agreed to meet and chat. We got along fairly well and within a couple of days we started working on his book project. It was a welcome diversion that lasted for a few months. He had already scribbled dozens of pages that ricocheted associatively through his acting career. We worked on honing his manuscript by giving it a more unified structure and trying to find a voice that captured the barbed humour that's always present when you're chatting with him. When I told Eric about Vivian and the role *Little Blue* had played in her life, I could tell that he was moved, even though he contends the series is lacklustre. He's welcome to his opinion, even if it is the wrong one.

Eric stopped drinking coffee shortly after *Little Blue* ended. While collaborating on his book, I dramatically increased my own intake of caffeine. One afternoon, Eric surprised and delighted me by quoting Oliver Kim cautioning Derek Hands against his excessive coffee consumption. I got the message and tapered myself to a couple of cups a day. If Viv had been there, she would have levitated out of her chair to hear Eric quote Oliver. Sigh. I had to bite my tongue frequently to stop myself from talking too much about Viv around him. But we were working on the Eric Minor Book Project, not the Vivian Cloze Book Project.

I'm thrilled to say that Eric has generously agreed to let me reproduce the chapter on *Little Blue* from his memoir, *Minor Characters*. (Thank you, Eric!)

"My Life as Derek Hands" by Eric Minor

Jason Bloch thinks he's a genius. He isn't. He's a coward and a weenie. I saw a bumper sticker the other day that said, "It takes balls to juggle." Let's just say he isn't much of a juggler.

Unfortunately, I didn't realize what a fraud he was until I saw the first episode of *Little Blue.* He hovers around creative people and traps their ideas in his little butterfly net. Then he uses these ideas and calls them his own. Despite what the credits say, *Little Blue* was not "created, written, and directed by Jason Bloch." Yes, the initial blip for the series came from him, but most of his ideas after that first blip were flimsy.

For starters, let's look at the character I played on *Little Blue*, Derek Hands.

I can easily list every idea for the character of Derek that came from Bloch:

1. That he would wear those god-awful mustard-yellow pants.

At one point, Bloch abandoned the set for a few days to examine colour swatches. He came back with colours that defined each character. Mine was mustard yellow. When I first slipped on the piss-coloured pants, I asked him, "Am I playing a hand of bananas?" One of his assistants giggled.

2. The pencil moustache.

For some reason, Bloch decided that every male character on the show had to have a moustache. One day during prep, another one of his assistants handed me a photocopy of an image of Little Richard. She said, "Jason needs you to grow this moustache for the project." There was a red arrow pointing at Little Richard's pencil moustache. When I asked her why, she shrugged. Typical Bloch. Have your cute assistant deliver some news so you don't have to answer any pesky questions.

3. Derek's nonsensical catchphrase "Well played, sir," which has haunted me ever since.

Bloch was fond of filming dozens of takes for a particular scene. As an actor, this approach worried me. It suggests that the director doesn't know what he wants, and that he's looking for options he can use later in the editing room. It also makes it really difficult for me to control my performance. Maybe the director will choose the take where I smiled too widely or said a line that had been thrown at me from off camera. That's exactly what happened with the line "Well played, sir." During one scene in the diner, Bloch solicited lines for my character from the cast and crew. He called this technique "spitballing," a slang term he borrowed from baseball. There were a number of suggestions and we tried them all. They took a few close-ups of me saying this line and sprinkled them into different episodes to make it one of Derek's verbal tics. Many people have inquired if Derek is meant to have a few loose wires, and I've always said that I wasn't playing him that way, though it may have been Bloch's secret intention for the character.

4. The nickname Lefty.

When the name Lefty was "spitballed" at me, I refused to say it because it made no sense. "My friends call me Lefty." Derek Hands was right handed, and what right-handed person goes by the nickname Lefty? I resisted saying the line. Filming stalled briefly. Bloch sulked and fumed. Finally, Ricky Jay broke the standstill. "Are you seriously going to hold us hostage? Is that what you were brought here to do? Just say the line so we can break for some shrimp cocktail." I said the line and Ricky Jay got his shrimp cocktail.

Those four ideas compose everything Jason Bloch contributed to my character and the last two ideas didn't even come directly from him.

I wanted to play nineteenth-century French writer Honoré de Balzac on the show. That's why my character drank so much coffee. He was emulating Balzac, who drank dozens of cups of coffee a day to churn out his novels. I was even learning to speak French and gaining weight to prepare for the role. Bloch put the brakes on me playing Balzac and asked me to come up with a different character. When *Little Blue* finally aired, I saw that sixteenth-century astronomer Tycho Brahe was a character. And he spoke Danish. I wonder how that gold-plated butterfly landed in Bloch's net.

I've worked with plenty of people with far more talent

than Jason Bloch. Last year, I had the pleasure of working with director David Gordon Green on the Seth Rogen–penned stoner spy comedy *James Bong*. The talents of David Gordon Green, Seth Rogen, and James Franco dwarf those of Jason Bloch. They are not intimidated by others' ideas and create a safety net of camaraderie rather than a butterfly net of trickiness. When I surprised them by stuttering during my scene with Franco, they were delighted. "A stuttering blackjack dealer!" Seth roared. He turned to Dave and declared, "I love this guy!" This was more praise than I received during the entire filming of *Little Blue*. The only problem was that Franco kept cracking up every time I asked him, "Another c-c-c-c-c-card, sir?" A much better problem to have than pettiness. In Franco's defence, this scene was shot towards the end of a long day and he might have eaten one too many brownies by then.

While filming *Little Blue*, I drank endless cups of coffee. Before leaving in the morning, I would drink an entire pot of coffee. On set, I'd hit craft services and fill my travel mug with more coffee. I barely ate anything—a jelly donut here, a chocolate croissant there, a piece of fruit from time to time. Coffee and pastries and water. The trick was to maintain a steady hum of caffeine flowing through me. It made me fairly agitated the entire time, but I was committed to the role of Derek Hands, and Derek, in turn, was committed to caffeine. Derek had taken caffeine as his sacrament. It was his cult, his religion. That's why I wore the VITAMIN BRO 12 T-shirt. It was a nod to cult leader Brother XII, who briefly lived on Cruikshank Island, where we filmed the show. That's why I told Timmy Whiffle that I was "profoundly caffeinated like Honoré de Balzac." To which Timmy snickered, "Honour thy ball sack, Hands. Honour thy ball sack."

I think the fans of the show who have watched it

countless times have started seeing things that aren't there. The ones I've talked to actually think it makes sense. It doesn't. They seem to think Bloch crafted every frame of the show like an expert watchmaker squinting through a jeweller's eyepiece to assemble the delicate pieces inside. Sorry to say it, but it was not like that. He was fumbling along and any depth you might see to the show is imaginary, like someone who can still feel their amputated leg when there's nothing there. One of Bloch's talents (for the first few years, at least) was to surround himself with brilliant creative types. It's not that difficult to make something compelling when you have the best cinematographer, editor, composer, et cetera. But when you don't have a structure to hang everything on, you're sunk. On the surface everything looks solid, but when you go deeper into it, you come up short, like biting into a hollow chocolate bunny.

It pains me to admit it, but there were glimmers of greatness on *Little Blue*. The crew was embarrassingly good, especially Chris Doyle. He may have been half-corked on set, but hand the man a camera and he turns into a fucking alchemist. For all its flaws, *Little Blue* looks gorgeous. And the cast was solid.

The point is nothing good on the show came from Bloch. It was the work of someone else. If you want to see his true talent, go watch his masterpiece, *Chimney Peep*. Unlike *Little Blue*, it was undoubtedly "written and directed by Jason Bloch." Here, you see his true intellectual heft because he failed to surround himself with smart people with good ideas he could steal.

Chimney Peep stars Tom Green as a three-foot-tall chimney sweep named Sir Humpsalot, who is also a peeping tom. Plus, it's a musical. I've got to admit that Bloch really outdid himself with ditties like "Jerkin' Me Gherkin," which a soot-covered Green sings in full cockney accent while rubbing his enormous codpiece. Not surprisingly, the film was eviscerated by critics. My favourite review was all pith and vinegar: "Jason Bloch, I demand that you forfeit your 'genius' grant, you depraved charlatan. You have created the shittiest film I've ever seen."

Creating a backstory for whatever character you're embodying is essential. It may be difficult to tell because so much of my work on *Little Blue* ended up in the rubbish bin, but I knew everything about Derek Hands from soup to nuts. Even when I played Blackjack Dealer #2 in *James Bong*, I created an intricate backstory for him. I knew that his stutter disappeared briefly while he worked with a kind-hearted speech pathologist named Emily. It returned when she left town to follow her lover, a cruel glass-blower named Rodney. Some people would suggest that none of this backstory was necessary for the role, but I'd argue that it adds resonance to my only line in the film. And my distinctive stuttering, which only emerged while I added layers to the character of Keith Grice (aka Blackjack Dealer #2), clearly made an impression on the minds behind *James Bong*.

My biggest regret about working on *Little Blue* is that it ended my relationship with my girlfriend, Aubrey. Before then, we had always been as fizzy as root beer. I never told Bloch, but the main reason I wanted to play writer Honoré de Balzac was that Aubrey was born in the small town of Balzac, Alberta. I wanted to immortalize my love for her through my performance.

Aubrey had never been around me when I immersed myself in creating a role and I think everything would have been fine if Bloch hadn't continued to obstruct and baffle me at every turn. At the end of the day, I'd return home crestfallen and agitated. The twenty to thirty cups of coffee I drank a day weren't helping, but they were necessary to my process. Aubrey grew frustrated with me constantly railing against Bloch and the project. Before I knew it, she flew out to spend time with her sister in Medicine Hat. By the time *Little Blue* aired, Aubrey had already moved in with a laid-back museum curator. I'd spent months crafting a complex character for the woman I loved and he had been disfigured on the operating table.

A nd that, my friends, was Eric Minor, a fine actor and a gifted raconteur. For the record, my favourite performance of Eric's is his voice work as slippery-tongued dentist Dr. Eucalyptus on the animated series *Mary Canary*. "Yes, my goose, you do have a loose tooth. But, in truth, I can't soothe your mouth." One of the joys of working on *Minor Characters* with Eric was delving into his oeuvre.

When I'd seen too much *Little Blue* and needed a different televisual pick-me-up, I turned to *Mary Canary*. It could calm me when things seemed to be going off the rails. It felt like a thirty-minute-long animated hug. When I got home from work today, I watched an episode of *Mary Canary* to calm myself after being misgendered while buying groceries and again while getting a takeaway burrito. I corrected the grocery store cashier and she apologized; I didn't even bother correcting the bro at the burrito joint. Even when folks correct themselves, it still stings like a tiny plastic toothpick sword jabbed in my heart. And it just kind of stays there and I feel its sharpness for a while before it eventually dissolves. There's no need to say "sir" when I'm buying a cup of coffee. "How can I help you?" or "How can I help you today?" works just as well as "How can I help you, sir?" And, really, nobody thinks, "Goddamn, that cashier called me 'sir'! Just like Paul McCartney! Fuckin' A!"

Normally, I can weather being misgendered and just get on with my day after a brief sulk. This time it sent me into a tailspin. There's a gentle balancing act between the way I want to look and the way I need to look to be seen the way I need to be seen. I tend to be most comfortable in jeans, a T-shirt, and no makeup, but I recognize that strangers need certain visual cues to see me as a woman. Even adding a scarf or a necklace to my outfit increases the likelihood that I'll be seen as a woman.

Anyway, I put on an episode of *Mary Canary* to elevate my mood. It wasn't the episode with Eric's amazing appearance as Dr. Eucalyptus. This was the episode with Ella the Umbrella's story of how she broke one of her metallic ribs during a storm and was cast in a gutter. As soon as she started describing the early days of her unlikely friendship with Tanis the Tennis Shoe, I received a text from my friend Nora who said she was on a first date at a coffee shop nearby. The date wasn't going well and she asked if I wanted to hang out. I texted back, Yes!!! and added an emoji of a smiling cat with heart eyes.

A few minutes later, I let her into my apartment. "What a cocksuck day," she said. "I need a drink." She draped her white leather jacket over a chair by the door.

Nora is a cute, foul-mouthed pastry chef with a dramatic, asymmetrical haircut who rides a motorcycle. I've described her to more than one person as a sheep in wolf's clothing. She carries herself like a badass, but she's incredibly sweet.

I opened a bottle of wine and filled a couple of teacups. Nora started talking about her daydream of starting a trans femme militia. Clearly, things had not gone well on the date.

I should mention that Nora is only interested in guys for sex and only when she needs to get (to quote her) "banged out." Even with her heightened libido, this guy had missed the mark by a wide margin. And now she was drinking red wine from a floral teacup and conspiring to start an underground militia composed of trans women. Nora, being trans and Chinese, deals with a fucked-up Venn diagram of oppression. She argued that any marginalized group that's treated horribly will eventually rebel and fight back. She had a point.

"Did you read that article on bonobos?" she asked. "Females wear the crown in those communities. The women will band together and attack a male bonobo who wrongs one of them. They'll even bite off body parts. The other male bonobos will just stand back and watch because they don't want to be attacked. That's what we need to do. These cis dudes have no fucking idea how powerful we are."

After refilling our little teacups, I put an album on the turntable that Nora had mentioned a few months ago. It was a compilation of obscure Belgian electronic music from the early nineties. Before I knew it, we were making out. It's surprising how my body is smarter than me. It seemed to know this was going to happen and was totally receptive. If I'd known this was a possibility, I would have been so nervous. I'd actually been crushing on Nora ever since I met her through Viv.

I hadn't made out with anyone for months and I'd really missed being touched. A vague emotional ache I'd had seemed to blossom and melt, blossom and melt. I hadn't really noticed the ache until now. It was like turning your head and noticing something in a blind spot that had been there for a long time. It was like diving into a pool and realizing you hadn't swum in way too long and loved the freedom of being in the water. Scratch that. It was so much better than swimming. I felt myself pulled into a rush of lips and curves and hands and softness and desire. There are so many delightful things bodies can do together. We did some of them.

When I went to pee, I saw a smear of Nora's bright red lipstick on my mouth in the bathroom mirror. It reminded me of Vivian's favourite shade of lipstick. My eyes welled with tears. I locked the door and wept. I've never been a silent crier, and soon Nora knocked, asking if I was okay. Rather than pretending, I opened the door and told her that I missed Vivian. She folded me in her arms and held me for a long time. It was sweet and awkward.

I i

INKY is the Gorses' piebald horse. When she is distraught, Melanie Gorse retreats to the barn to brush Inky. Without her parents' knowledge, Melanie is teaching Inky a musical freestyle routine to the song "Rebirth of Slick (Cool Like Dat)" by Digable Planets. Inky has perfected a dope on-the-beat head nod, but she struggles with learning to do the robot, possibly because her tail won't stop twitching.

While sifting through Viv's belongings with Dot, I opened a small box that contained a couple of bushy tails and several smooth objects, some of them metallic. Whoa, I thought, Viv owned quite a few butt plugs. I wondered how hygienic the ones with tails were. One looked like a red fox tail and the other looked like a raccoon tail. They looked like real fur, even though I'm sure they were synthetic. They were incredibly cute and the animal lover in me wanted to touch them, but that would be so strange. The metallic ones were smooth and shiny and also wanted to be touched.

It's surreal to see your distorted reflection in your best friend's polished steel butt plug. I wondered how many of these toys were gifts from men she'd dated. And I wondered how long people have been putting objects in their butts. After putting Viv's butt toys in the pile of things that would go in the trash, I kept expecting to happen upon other sex toys or some porn. I discovered a couple tubes of lube, but that was all. It looked like her collection of sexy objects was focussed entirely on her butt.

I wasn't sure if I was crossing some invisible line by writing about Viv's butt toys. But when I talked to Dot, she said that her sister would have wanted to be seen for who she was. Viv got to a place where she wasn't embarrassed by her body or by wanting to explore it by herself and with lovers. She wasn't a kink evangelist; she just wasn't willing to be ashamed. She saw herself as loveable, desirable, and fuckable. I envied her sexual confidence.

Okay, I'll admit that I couldn't resist touching the raccoon tail. And the fox tail. And one of the polished metal plugs. It was so smooth, shiny, and heavy. Afterwards, I washed my hands like a doctor scrubbing for surgery.

Fine, I'll also admit that I felt the urge to purchase one of the metallic plugs for myself. It came in an adorable gift box, resting on a bed of crushed pink satin like it was a piece of jewellry. Until opening the box, I hadn't noticed how similar the shape of the plug was to a soother for an infant. It had a little ring for holding and a bulbous end for, uh, soothing. I will further admit that I now get Viv's obsession with steel butt plugs. They have a weight and a fullness that's lovely. And there's such a gentle pressure that you can just go about your day with it in place. You could even write for a few hours with that fullness and weight slowly doing their thing.

I wonder if I should simply delete the entire passage on butt toys, but I feel like I've crossed a threshold and am less ashamed of being a woman who happens to be trans and enjoys having toys in her ass. I know Viv would be delighted to see me finally reaching a place of less shame. In retrospect, I can see that one of the reasons she paid so much attention to me was that I was so shy and uncomfy in my skin.

I met Viv before I transitioned and she immediately took me under her wing. The days we spent wandering the city and talking were crucial for me accepting being trans. At the time, I was living with Ramona and going through my "gender-punk" phase, wearing more femme accessories. I might have framed it as "troubling gender norms." Ramona alternated between being amused by and tolerating my fashion choices. When I eventually told her that I was trans, it wasn't something she could handle. At first, she could. Then, she couldn't. She wanted to be supportive, but she felt betrayed and confused. When we moved in together, she didn't think she was making a life with another woman. I got it and felt guilty. Viv was a sweetheart; she offered to let me stay on the couch of her tiny shared apartment while I found a place for myself. The only other person who I might have stayed with was Christopher, but he kept his distance and didn't offer. He was still coming to terms with me being trans and didn't know

what to say or do around me, so he said nothing, did nothing.
Viv invited me in and kept me from getting too down.

J j

Ranjit JHA works at the Little Blue Soda Company and is widely considered to be the most beautiful woman on the island. She remains convinced that her beloved Captain Alphonse will return to her, even though he vanished the day after their son Tristan spoke his first word ("dada"). She deftly turns down Ian Earl Stairs as he clumsily woos her.

"

RANJIT: I'm sorry, Ian. I still love Captain Alphonse.
IAN: But he's a dirty disappearing dog.

RANJIT: You may be right. But we love the dog we
love, dirt and all.

"

Vivian loved that line: "But we love the dog we love, dirt and
all." It could have been her mantra. She loved a lot of dogs,
and nearly every one of her beaus had muddy, matted fur and
a wandering eye.

I once saw Padma Lakshmi, who plays Ranjit Jha, in a
gourmet sandwich shop downtown. She was almost unfath-
omably gorgeous. I couldn't help staring at her for a few seconds while she bit into her sandwich. I ordered the same one
she was eating—with pear and prosciutto—and stole a couple of glances of her while waiting for my order. When they
finally handed me the sandwich wrapped in butcher paper,
I walked past her briskly and she looked up at me for a second and raised her eyebrows. I almost fainted. According to
the internet, she must have been in town filming a romantic comedy called *Pink Leaves*. I watched it. It's not great, but
Padma is enchanting as a stylish, klutzy florist.

Tristan JHA attends kindergarten at Little Blue School. His
obsession with dolphins leads to the uncomfortable moment
when Ian Earl Stairs, trying to win the affection of Ranjit,
bursts into Tristan's class to awkwardly give him a wind-up
mechanical dolphin.

Tristan's best friend is Pauline Elder. Every day after
school, they watch a show about adventurous frozen mice
called *Ice Mice* while Pauline's father Roy Spittle paints.
During the show's catchy theme song, they bounce on the
couch and sing along, while her dog Visconti barks and wags
his tail. Even Viv couldn't help singing the show's theme song
in her typical off-key fashion.

Ice mice! Ice mice! We are ice mice!
Ice Abe! Ice Bert! Ice Cap! Ice mice!
We are, we are, we are ice mice!

Lady JOSEPHINE, Agnes Pennypacker's rambunctious sidekick, is one of the cutest dogs you'll ever see. I'm a cat person, but Lady Josephine is an irresistible doggie. Thanks to the Internet Movie Animal Database, I know that she is an Australian Shepherd. As I type this, I can imagine myself twenty years from now, living in a cabin on an island, going for long walks with my protective, affectionate Australian Shepherd. I have no idea how I'll make this a reality because most journalists aren't rolling in dough, but a tiny part of me knows that I'll be a spectacular old flannel-clad dyke with a gorgeous dog.

If you spend hundreds of hours with someone, you have a catalogue of tiny memories. As you live your life, those tiny memories snap and crackle your synapses. It can be overwhelming, like the world is already overlaid with experience. When I was picking up a lightbulb in the drugstore today, I was reminded of being in the exact same store with Viv while she filled a basket with twenty or thirty items. I had to carry some of her things because her basket was overflowing. She would keep a running list of what she needed from different stores and wait until she'd run out of something she couldn't do without. In this case, I think it was toothpaste. Whatever it was, she made the trip worthwhile by gathering dozens of items. Running errands with Viv was not for the faint hearted. That was the day when I discovered that she loved rice pudding. She grabbed several small tubs and plunked them in her basket. It had always seemed like such a plain dessert item to me until I saw how gaga for rice pudding Viv was. I helped carry her groceries home and she rewarded me by giving me a tube of her favourite drugstore lipstick. I tried looking for it recently, but they've stopped making it in Viv's signature shade. You can still order it from people who stockpiled it before it was discontinued. It's called Bloodshot Sighs.

I first met Nora at a protest that I went to with Vivian. About a hundred of us were gathered outside the downtown campus of the same university where I'd just finished my art history degree. We were protesting a talk at the university by a (so-called) feminist who spends much of her time arguing that trans women aren't women. I thought about those isolated Japanese soldiers hiding in the jungle who didn't know World War II had ended decades earlier.

Before we left the house, Viv told me that she wouldn't let anything happen to me.

"I might be smaller than you," she said, "but I will fuck up anyone who fucks with you. I am a femme Rottweiler, babe. Rawr!"

"I don't think Rottweilers roar," I said. "They bark."

"Fuck that," she said. "I'm a femme Rottweiler and I roar, bitch." She made her hands into claws and showed me her teeth. "Now let's go protest some backwards bullshit."

Vivian introduced me to a number of her friends at the protest, including Nora. I was still in my genderpunk phase at the time. Viv told me Nora had asked her to come inside the event with her for a few minutes. She wanted to know how I felt about going with her. If I didn't want to go, Viv wouldn't go. I didn't really want to go into the event we were protesting, but I said we should because I really didn't want Nora to go by herself.

We sank into seats at the back of the room, just as the doors were being closed. I had no idea why we were there. I felt like a fly that had just landed in a hornet's nest. Nothing good could come from being there. But there we were. Viv took my hand in hers. She smiled. She whispered in my ear, "Everything is fine, babe. I'm here." Viv's hand felt warm.

The event started with someone speaking into a microphone, thanking us for coming. I wondered how long we were going to stay. When the speaker paused to take a drink from her glass of water, Nora stood up.

"I might be at the wrong talk," Nora said loudly.

"Excuse me?" the woman with the microphone said, squinting to see who Nora was.

"I said that I might be at the wrong talk," Nora said again, even more loudly. "I thought this talk was going to include instructions on how to build a time machine. Are you going to talk about how to build a time machine?"

"Can someone get security," said the woman with the microphone, visibly flustered.

Nora continued, clearly and loudly: "Because I think you're going to NEED a time machine to get back to the bad old days of second-wave feminism. We exist. And we're not going anywhere."

Then she hustled us out of the room asap and slipped out through a side exit before security could arrive to put us in our place.

"Nora, that was fucking AMAZING," Viv said.

Nora led us to a place a few blocks away where she knew the bartender. We had our first drinks of the night. After a few more drinks and a side order of deep-fried pickles, we went for poutine because Nora was having a craving. Only then did I realize that Viv was a vegetarian and that vegetarian poutine existed. The night ended with the three of us sharing a drunk 2 a.m. banana split at Denny's. Eventually, I taxied home and stumbled into bed beside my exasperated girlfriend, Ramona. The next day, I told her I was trans.

Alison KIM works at Little Blue Diner, which her parents own. She is dating Thurman Park and has a world-weariness that you don't always see in people a year or two out of high school. We never see her discussing it with Thurman, but she seems to plan to attend university in Hawai'i. This isn't stated explicitly, but the envelope she drops at the post office in the ninth episode is addressed to the Office of Admissions at the University of Hawai'i at Mānoa.

Diane KIM owns and runs the diner with her husband, Oliver. She seems to be the only member of the family who has mastered the restaurant's antique cash register. After helping her daughter Tracy with her homework on malaria, Diane becomes obsessed with learning about parasites. For some reason, she feels compelled to share parasitic tidbits she has unearthed, regardless of the situation. Diane makes so many faux pas, such as when she warns Rusty Odell, who is trying to dig into a slice of rhubarb pie, that he could become infected with hookworm larvae if he touches his cat Dimple's feces. Rusty nods and nibbles on small forkfuls of pie.

But Diane's pièce de résistance of parasitology happens when Thurman Park arrives for a date with Alison.

"

DIANE: Did you know, Thurman, that queen bees mate with ten to twenty males even though it increases their chances of a predatory attack?

THURMAN: Uh, no.

DIANE: Do you know why they do that?

THURMAN: No, I don't know.

DIANE: The queen is making sure there is genetic diversity in her offspring so they're less susceptible to parasites. That's why she mates with so many males instead of one lucky little boy bee. Isn't that fascinating?

THURMAN: Uh, yes.

DIANE: Where are you and Alison going tonight?

THURMAN: A movie. We're going to see a movie. "

Oliver KIM saved for years to buy a jukebox for the diner that he crammed with original soul 45s. Diane quips that as soon as they landed on the island Oliver must have been infected with the jukebox parasite. One of my favourite moments of the series happens when the song "I Got a Sure Thing" by Ollie & the Nightingales plays on the jukebox. Oliver Kim walks away from the kitchen, bellowing "All hands on deck!" This prompts dishwasher Derek Hands to take over the grill for the next two minutes and thirty-five seconds. Oliver then serenades Diane while singing into a spatula. Alison rolls her eyes. When Oliver reaches the line about what his wife will do for him (rub his back, make him dinner, draw him a bath), Diane theatrically waves her hand and declares "Not tonight!" When the song ends, Oliver grins sheepishly, mimes tipping a hat, and bows deeply. In *Carter Exby Bulletin*, Lucy Six mentioned that Stanley Fine's only stipulation to Jason Bloch when he funded *Little Blue* was that it had to include soul music in some way. Enter the character of Oliver Kim.

Tracy KIM works part-time at the family restaurant, where she seems to spend much of her time memorizing Lady Macbeth's lines for a scene she will be performing in Mr. Bits's English class with Mitch Marberry and Emmanuel Curwood. Tracy surprises Delia and Ren Crease when they enter the diner for the first time and she greets them with the lines, "Sit, worthy friends; my lord"—pointing at Oliver—"is often thus, / And hath been from his youth. Pray you, keep seat."

" TRACY: Think of this, good peers, / But as a thing of custom: 'tis no other; / Only it spoils the pleasure of the time.
DIANE: What man dare, I dare: / Come thou like the rugged Russian bear, / The arm'd —
OLIVER: It is a tale told by an idiot, full of sound and fury and sautéed onions!

DIANE: Oliver!

TRACY: Dad!

DIANE: You are an idiot. Be careful with that spatula, Romeo.

OLIVER: That which we call a spatula / By any other name would flip as sweetly.

TRACY: You have displaced the mirth, broke the good meeting, / With most unwelcome disorder.

OLIVER: Ha! The Lady Macbeth doth rehearse too much, methinks.

"

Later, we see Tracy's unbelievable talent show routine. It is breathtaking to watch her walk onto the gymnasium stage wearing a straightjacket and stand under a banner reading, "Failure means a drowning death!" The judges are visibly confused because this wasn't the talent she'd exhibited during rehearsals. She is quickly lowered into a tall milk canister that is then padlocked. I still find myself holding my breath during the long, silent moment while we watch the motionless canister onstage with the foreboding banner hanging above it. When Tracy finally emerges free from the straightjacket and covered in milk, I am able to exhale. Viv loved this scene, but she found the pause before Tracy reappears unbearably long. "C'mon," she would murmur. "C'mon, c'mon, c'mon, get out, c'mon, hurry."

I didn't really think about race on *Little Blue* until I went with Viv to a convention for fans of the show. During the convention, we attended a talk by Claire Kubo and Jay Ryu. Their talk about racialized characters on *Little Blue* illuminated aspects of the show that had been invisible to me earlier.

After their talk, I delved into their website, the Little Blue Soda Company, which often highlights race on the series.

At the outset of their talk, Claire and Jay stated that one of the things that first drew them to *Little Blue* was its abundance of Asian characters. They recounted the lack of Asian representation on television in 2001, when *Little Blue* aired, mentioning a few examples of characters from the time, including the hypersexual villainous character Lucy Liu played on *Ally McBeal*, and Keiko Agena, who played the best friend character on *Gilmore Girls*. (When I started taking femme pills, I decided to immerse myself in shows about young women going through puberty, which had been suggested by another trans woman in my support group. It was a dynamite idea. One of the first shows I watched was *Gilmore Girls*, which is so soothing it's like sinking into a bubble bath. After we watched *Little Blue* together the first time, I tried to get Viv to watch *Gilmore Girls* with me, but she quickly decided it wasn't for her.)

Little Blue features nine Asian characters, which was unprecedented at the time. Plus, there were three Black characters. Claire and Jay emphasized that none of these twelve characters seems to be rooted in racial stereotypes. None of them has an exaggerated accent or is shoehorned in to provide comic relief.

Claire and Jay have discussed how monumental it was for a dozen BIPOC actors to be given the leeway to develop their own characters, to make their characters as idiosyncratic as they wanted. Two of the most beloved characters on the series are Roy Spittle and Sherman Park.

The only directions Jason Bloch gave to actor Archie West, who played Roy Spittle, was that his character would have a horseshoe-shaped moustache, wear a dark green blazer, and have a daughter. At the time, West had only acted in one or two local indie films and was just starting to make a living as an artist. In an interview about the genesis of Roy, West talked about how he "wanted to show a Black artist creating art in front of the camera." He continued: "Most of the Black actors on TV then [in the late nineties and early aughts] were on sitcoms or crime shows. I'd had enough of that." He repeated one of the mantras Jason Bloch often told actors during the development process: "Find your character's obsession and zero in on it."

Archie West's obsession became Alma Thomas, an unheralded African American painter. In particular, he found himself zeroing in on her painting *Starry Night and the Astronauts*. West explains, "Mostly, it's blue splotches of paint all up and down the canvas. And then, up there, up in the corner, you've got these splotches of different colours. Red splotches. Orange splotches. And yellow splotches. That was the moment for me. Red, orange, yellow. Roy G. Biv. That's it, I thought. And the character of Roy started to open up for me."

Sherman Park is undoubtedly my favourite character on *Little Blue*. Sherman is brilliantly played by actor/musician Ji-young Yoon. Yoon, who now identifies as nonbinary, immigrated to Calgary with their family when they were three years old. At the time *Little Blue* was filmed, Yoon was a dapper trans man living in East Vancouver and playing in an indie folk band. All of these qualities found their way into Sherman. Apparently, Jason Bloch told Yoon that their character's defining colour would be royal purple, that they played bass guitar in a band (Yoon had played guitar during the audition process), and their name would be Sherman. Yoon did the rest, having Sherman in many ways emulate Prince. As Yoon later remarked, "Looking back, that's probably what Jason wanted me to do when he told me that I was playing a musician and told me Sherman's colour was royal purple, right?" To add a little panache to the character, Yoon decided Sherman would work in a candy store that only played bubblegum music. Says Yoon, "Sherman is basically my dream of what would happen if Prince and Willy Wonka had a love child." Yoon once confessed to wanting to make Sherman a "sexy motherfucker." Mission accomplished.

Claire and Jay's profile of Sherman on their website emphasizes how truly subversive Yoon's character was. When *Little Blue* aired, there was only one openly trans actor in South Korea, and she had only come out as trans a few months earlier. "At the time," they write, "it was almost unheard of in South Korea to legally change your gender marker. And here comes Ji-young Yoon playing a magnetic trans guy who instantly seduces us. The character of Sherman changed the lives of a lot of LGBTQ fans, especially Koreans."

Viv and I went to see Ji-young Yoon's band the Sour Capes a couple of years ago at a club downtown. Ji-young was one of the most energetic forty-year-olds I've ever seen, bouncing and whirling around onstage like they'd just turned twenty.

In one post on their Little Blue Soda Company site, Claire and Jay list all of the characters we see on the show by race, which is a good visual reminder of the whiteness of most residents on Little Blue Island. Elsewhere, Claire and Jay have pointed out that the series includes no acknowledgement of racism or even of race in any of its episodes. Although racism is never discussed on the show, they have pointed to overt examples of it, including Freddy Gorse's bullying of Tristan Jha and Ian Earl Stairs's entitled pursuit of Ranjit Jha. They have also foregrounded that the racialized characters mostly stick together. For example, Tristan Jha's best friend is Pauline Elder, the only other kid of colour in his kindergarten class. Meanwhile, Roy Spittle's best friend, poetic tugboat driver

Dalton Fludd, is the only other Black adult on the series. The three members of Teach Yourself Beekeeping (Herman, Sherman, and Thurman Park) live together, and so do the only other four Korean characters on the series: the Kims, who run Little Blue Diner. They also lamented that there were no Indigenous characters on the series, even though it was set and filmed on Cruikshank Island, where members of the W̱SÁNEĆ and W̱JOȽEȽP First Nations have fished and lived for thousands of years.

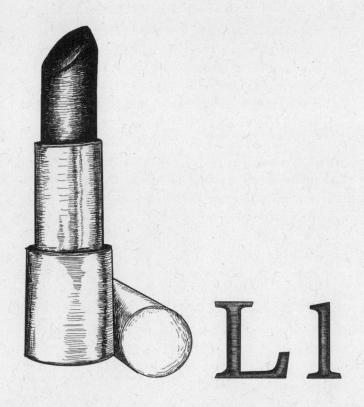

Ll

Isobel LACROIX owns Little Blue Bookstore and has lived on the island longer than anyone else. She seems to know where every book is located among the stacks and stacks of books heaped on the floor throughout her store. She doesn't hide her disdain for the island's richest resident, Roderick Ambleside. Still an excellent swimmer, she once swam to the mainland to win a wager with Roderick's father, Chappy. She's had insomnia for many years and has grown dependent on sleeping pills.

When Dalton Fludd stumbles on an unexploded bomb, Isobel is the character who explains that it's a prop from a movie that was filmed on Little Blue Island in the sixties. Isobel claims to have appeared onscreen briefly in the background as a cigarette girl showing off her "glorious gams." The film was a comedy called *Bumf*. It was set in World War II and its humour revolved around a toilet-paper shortage.

After making out with Nora that first time, we started getting together occasionally. Before long, I realized that this wasn't enough for me. I'd need to start dating again. I still cried sometimes when we got together, but queer women are pretty understanding about crying after (or even while) making out.

I joined an online dating site that had been mentioned by a few friends. I set up my account, answered a handful of questions, uploaded an image and started browsing the profiles of other queer women who might be good "matches" for me. It was weird, especially because I wasn't even sure exactly what I wanted. Did I want a relationship? Did I care if they were involved with someone else? Did I need to get along with them or was my body just looking for another body to do things with? How many of these women would want to make out with a trans lesbian? Why couldn't more of them choose better images for their profile? Why did I lose interest in women who were fans of terrible pop culture? Why was I so bothered when someone listed one of the things they're "good at" as sex? What would that woman think of my body? How should I frame myself in my profile? Did I look too soft butch in my image? Could I make out with someone who was inarticulate? How could I appear interesting and desirable without also seeming desperate or braggy?

During the first couple of weeks on the site, my emotional EKG spiked and dipped more than I care to admit. I was back in junior high, passing notes to cute girls, waiting to see if they'd respond. The hardest thing was tussling with my emotions, trying to keep dips to a minimum. For the most part, things happened very slowly. I took to describing the women I interacted with on the site as "cute queer sloths." I met a few of them for coffee and was surprised at how often textual chemistry didn't translate to sexual chemistry. You can exchange messages and images and seem to really like each other, but when you meet in person that's often pretty irrelevant. The one person I met and felt a pull towards worked in a lab at the same university where I was doing my (now paused) journalism grad degree. It's a small, queer world after all.

Ruby was cute, calm, and whip smart. It's tricky early on to suss out what cis women (in this case, Ruby) think it will be like making out with trans women (in this case, me). The first queer cis woman I dated after transitioning told me that for most of her friends and acquaintances the "babeliness" of trans and genderqueer folks was self-evident, which was lovely to hear, even if it hasn't turned out to be entirely accurate.

When Ruby wasn't working in the lab, she juggled a lot of other things: volunteering, rock climbing (!), playing keyboard in a queercore duo called Vulva Death Grip (!!) and dating her on-again, off-again girlfriend, Robin, who has one of the coolest haircuts ever (shaved here, dyed there, ever changing). Somehow, even with her overflowing schedule we managed to see each other at least once a week, and she always made me feel like she'd been looking forward to seeing me the entire time we'd been apart.

After we'd only been dating for a month or two, Ruby said to me matter-of-factly, "Vivian was the love of your life." She wasn't jealous; she just recognized something that I hadn't. I probably wobbled my head and said "maybe" before changing topics.

When I stayed with Vivian, I learned that she suffered from pattern baldness and rocked a variety of wigs. She looked stunning with her head shaved, but she was convinced that men wouldn't be attracted to her without hair. She always wore wigs, making sure to fasten them as securely as possible in case a nasty wind blew through her hair or a lover felt the urge to tug her hair in a fit of passion. When she went out drinking and dancing, she didn't want to risk damaging her everyday hair, so she'd wear cute, short synthetic hair that was a striking robin's-egg blue. (I quickly learned that she always called it her hair, rather than a wig.) Over time, I realized that she was incredibly distressed by her baldness, which had started afflicting her when she was in her teens. A mutual friend of ours once brought up the statistics for adult women with pattern baldness, but Viv wasn't reassured by the number of cis women around her who were also wearing hair that wasn't their own. Viv seemed so carefree and confident, but she always harboured the fear that her lovers would discover this secret and stop being attracted to her or, far worse, stop seeing her as a woman.

Judy MARBERRY is married to Stephen Marberry, and has two children, Mitch and Stephanie. She is a potter who specializes in teapots, though she is best known as the character who sings all of her dialogue. As with Tycho Brahe's dialogue in Danish, none of the other characters seem to notice that Judy sings rather than speaks. And most of her singing seems nonsensical. What is she going on about in the song "Jiminy Stitson Dood It"? It just raises several questions. Who is Jiminy Stitson? What did he do? What does it mean to have "dood" something rather than done it? But, really, these questions are pointless. Judy is effervescent. When Jason

Bloch was asked why all of Judy Marberry's dialogue was sung, he said, "Why would you cast Lina Smith and not let her sing?" I'm not a fan of musicals, but I've watched nearly every musical with Lina Smith in it. My favourite one is *My Gosh, My Ghost*. I particularly adore the way her voice cracks on the song "Mr. Syllable" when the ghost of her husband lets go of her hand on the rowboat.

Like Judy Marberry, Viv would sometimes break into weird little songs, as though she was living in a low-budget musical. One of the first times I visited her place, she suddenly started singing as I was lacing up my Docs to leave. "Boots awwwwwwn," she sang dramatically. "You gotta put your boots awwwwwwn." She paused. "Boots on for the poison ray-hey-hey-hain." She was fond of adding post-apocalyptic flourishes to liven things up.

Mitch MARBERRY is frequently seen cruising the town's main drag in his candy-apple-red muscle car alongside his girlfriend, Melanie Gorse. He keeps a bottle of ketchup in his car's glove compartment for Melanie, his "catsup-lovin' queen."

Even though she claimed to hate the baseball episode, Viv loved every moment with Mitch Marberry, especially the way he coaxes Melanie to blast his "walk-up song" from his car each time it's his turn to bat. The game would halt for a few moments while Robert Gordon's rockabilly version of "The Way I Walk" blared. (No other player had a "walk-up song.") Then, Mitch (batting average .049) would strike out after swinging at three terrible pitches and then sulk on the bench while restyling his post-batting-helmet pompadour (the first two times) or destroying a fence post with his baseball bat (the third time). Viv also loved how Mitch wore his leather jacket over his uniform the entire game.

He is also revealed to have a poor memory and an inability to break away from his usual fifties slang after he casts himself in the role of Macbeth for a performance with Emmanuel Curwood and Tracy Kim in Mr. Bits's English class. Can I just say I felt fairly melancholy when Mitch was demoted from Macbeth to playing the silent role of Banquo's ghost? Phrases like "dust this joint" and "move in the groove" never appeared in Shakespeare, Mitch. But, oh, how I wish they had. Props to Mitch for playing Banquo's ghost in his leather jacket.

> EMMANUEL: We should rehearse the play so we don't embarrass ourselves.
> MITCH: Cool it, nosebleed.
> EMMANUEL: What?
> MITCH: Just cool it. Dig?
> EMMANUEL: I hear you, but I don't want to look stupid.
> MITCH: Cut the gas, ghostboy. I'm the king of this thing.
> TRACY: Let's just relax. Don't get, uh, frosted, Mitch.
> MITCH: No sweat. I'm cool, baby.
> TRACY: Maybe we should do another table read with our scripts.
> MITCH: Boss idea. That's Fat City.

Viv found Mitch's awkward greaser persona adorable. She wanted to cuddle him like a tomcat that's been neutered and declawed.

Stephen MARBERRY is Roderick Ambleside's right-hand

man. It is implied that Stephen was the person who persuaded Tycho Brahe to relocate to Little Blue Island from Denmark to work for Roderick. After lovesick Tycho names a comet after his beloved May Underwood, we see Stephen calming down a furious Roderick, who reveals that he wanted to name it after himself.

Emmanuel Curwood's opening narration reveals that Judy and Stephen Marberry will be murdered by someone dressed in a bear costume. We never find out who murdered them, but we do learn that the police repeatedly question Emmanuel and that they later arrest a different suspect. There are plenty of theories about who killed them, with the most compelling one pointing to Mitch Marberry. Viv always suspected the killer was Timmy Whiffle. Her evidence was his "general shadiness" and his nonchalance at learning they were dead. Who hears two people in their small town were brutally murdered and says, "Bummer"?

Stephanie MARBERRY is Judy and Stephen's adopted daughter. She is treated horribly by her brother, Mitch, which belies the cuddliness Viv claimed to see in him. Mitch harasses Stephanie repeatedly, even though she's still clearly traumatized by the death of her best friend, Emma Curwood. The first time I watched *Little Blue* after Vivian died, I wept several times. I cry less now when I watch the series, but I do find myself tearing up whenever Stephanie is onscreen. Her grief is always apparent. Even her weak pommel horse routine at the talent show seems to be steeped in grief. When Stephanie Marberry wins top prize at the talent show (via her father's bribery), she walks over and gives her prize to Tracy Kim, acknowledging her spectacular, crowd-pleasing milk-canister escape act.

Dot had asked me if I'd wanted to say anything at Viv's funeral. I hadn't. I was worried about transforming into a six-foot-tall teardrop before dozens of sad strangers in folding chairs. They didn't need to watch me sob my way through a speech. At the funeral, so many of her friends spoke. They shared things I hadn't known about her. She'd played dodgeball on a team called Vamps + Tramps. She'd volunteered at a drop-in centre for sex workers. Dot revealed that Viv had been a gifted figure skater when she was young. I suddenly remembered how unfettered she'd always seemed on the dance floor. She moved with clarity and confidence. Dancing beside her, I always felt like the graceless dancer the choreographer couldn't fire from the company because she was the artistic director's niece. Even Viv's shy roommate Claudia got up to say a few words about how Viv had shown her how to do winged eyeliner and make perfect poached eggs. I should have said something. Viv had given me so much more than makeup tips. After the last speaker, they invited anyone who wanted to say anything about Viv to come up and speak. A few more of her friends went up and shared memories. I stayed in my folding chair, telling myself that if I got up I'd just ramble and blubber and tarnish everyone else's remembrances.

Nn

Tindra NORTH is one of the announcers during the base-ball game. Her role seems to be providing the colour commentary. Halfway through the game, she welcomes "all the baseball fans in White Peach," who were apparently watching another game that went into overtime, though it's unclear which network is broadcasting this game between the Little Blue Cubs and the Little Blue Bears. Tindra seems to have a crush on Roy Spittle. We never see her again after the base-ball episode.

Christopher had season tickets for a local minor league baseball team, and he took me to an afternoon game on a weekday. We arrived a little early and went to his reserved seats with our mustard-smeared hot dogs and plastic cups full of craft beer. He started badgering me about returning to school, and I told him that I'd be going back before long. Of course, he didn't appreciate it when I asked him when he would be returning to school. He had been studying business, but he'd lost interest halfway through his degree. I told him to get a BFA, which is what he wanted to do before our parents talked him out of it.

"My friend Lila is making a living from her art," I told him. I didn't mention that she was barely making ends meet.

He shrugged. I knew he was probably disappointed that I had asked Lila rather than him to do the illustrations for the encyclopedia. "How's your dating life?" he asked.

I wiped some mustard from my lips and started telling him about Ruby. He nodded, sipped some of his beer, and scanned the half-full stands around us. Typical Christopher. Ask a question and ignore the answer. I started dropping in words he couldn't ignore. Queer. Dyke. Nonmonogamous.

"Do you want another beer?" he asked. He waved over one of the roaming beer vendors. "Cheers, sis," he said. We raised our plastic beer cups. "I'm glad you could make it today."

I shifted my sitting position, wishing I'd remembered to bring a cushion. My ass was not going to be happy with me. I asked Chris if he was still dating Alice and he told me things hadn't worked out. He said he was going on a date in a few days with a woman who had her own webcomic. Her name was Tina, she wore glasses, and she worked in a shoe store downtown. That was everything he could tell me about her.

The game started, and we stopped talking for a while.

Our starting pitcher hit a batter, threw a couple of wild pitches, couldn't find the strike zone. I thought of Mr. Bits and his pitching woes. The opposing team scored a couple of runs quickly. Our team brought in another pitcher, who was only slightly better. The other team scored another couple of runs. Christopher brought up my short-lived career as a pitcher in little league. I'd only pitched two games. In the first one, I did fairly well. In the second game, I gave up a string of hits to the other team. Our dad was the coach. He walked out to the mound and told me that he wasn't going to bring in another pitcher. I had to pitch my way out of this inning. He wasn't going to throw me a life preserver. I had to swim to shore on my own. As he walked away from the pitcher's mound, it dawned on me that I was in control, that I could make him suffer more than he could make me suffer. He cared about baseball; I didn't. I started pitching like it was batting practice. The other team scored a few more runs before the inept fielders on my little league team finally managed to get the necessary three outs. As I walked off the field, my dad gave me a look of anger and disgust. Things were never rosy between us, but I generally tried to do what he wanted me to do because it was easier. Plus, I didn't like being on the receiving end of his anger. When he'd finished recapping for me the story of my life as an unsuccessful pitcher, Christopher said, "Dad was so fucking pissed at you, bro."

I reddened. "Bro," I repeated. "What the fuck, Chris."

He apologized and waved over the beer vendor. After the game, we went to a nearby artisanal ice cream shop. Christopher had burnt caramel, and I had whiskey hazelnut.

Rusty ODELL is the town's former lighthouse keeper and current ne'er-do-well. In his mid-fifties, Rusty is mistakenly thought by other islanders to be mute because he never speaks in front of them. He lives in the lighthouse, along with his cat, Dimple, who he reads to from the novel *Babewolf*. His best friend is Ian Earl Stairs, who gives him a free shave every morning. Despite his reputation as the town drunkard, we never see Rusty intoxicated or consuming alcohol. In fact, he seems especially fond of lemonade.

Vivian was also a serious lemonade fiend. The coffee shop she worked at was known for its pitchers of tart and tangy lemonade. She dated a few guys she met through the coffee shop, including one who even I liked. He was a regular who would get a small pitcher of lemonade and a cheese-and-bacon scone every morning. When he asked her out, Viv said she'd go if he'd settle for a cheese-and-chive scone instead. He agreed to take the vegetarian option for Viv and turned out to be clever and charming, albeit emotionally unavailable.

Shortly after Beyoncé released her visual album *Lemonade,* I saw videos for a few songs recreated by trans women. Their version of "Hold Up" is a masterpiece. It features a Black trans woman smashing car windows with a baseball bat named Hot Sauce. Game, set, and match. When I first heard the title of Beyoncé's album, I thought of Viv and her charming lemonade lover. When I saw the video with trans women and the shattered car windows, I knew Viv would lose her mind if she saw it. It wasn't Britpop, but it was a thousand shades of Oh My God, Yes.

In *Carter Exby Digest*, Lucy Six suggests that Rusty Odell was a draft dodger. Her evidence is pretty compelling: he reads aloud to Dimple with a strong accent that one expert calls "Pittsburg English"; he arrived on the island during the height of the Vietnam War; and his bookshelf includes a copy of *Manual for Draft-Age Immigrants to Canada*, an infamous "draft-dodging bible."

Rusty Odell was played by ginger-haired actor Hatch Robichaud, who has played two other characters named Rusty: Rusty Lossing, a clockmaker with a troubled past, in Esther Kellum's *International Air* (1998) and Rusty Tink, a colourblind blacksmith, in David Mamet's melodrama *West of Death* (2014).

Once when we were watching *Little Blue*, Viv paused the screen to linger on a shot of Dimple asleep in a bed of sunshine in the lantern room of the lighthouse. I thought we were taking a bathroom break, so I went to pee. When I came back, she played for me "the best Britpop song about lighthouses ever," which is "My Lighthouse" by Pulp. The narrator in the song takes someone up to his lighthouse and tries to sweet-talk them by displaying what could be theirs if they throw in their lot with him. I thought the lighthouse keeper in the song was wearing grandeur-tinted glasses. But Viv seemed to find it romantic.

"Where are all the hot lighthouse keepers?" she asked.

"Probably dead," I said.

"There are still lighthouses, so there have to be a few hot ones out there."

"Maybe try googling 'lighthouse keeper fuckboy' or go on Grindr," I said.

She laughed. "Lighthouse keeper fuckboy!? Who are you? Are you on Grindr?"

I shrugged.

"Are you?!" she asked.

"Maybe I should create a special Grindr account just for you: *lighthousefuckboy69*."

"I know you're kidding," she said. "But you're kinda turning me on. Fuck. Maybe I do have a lighthouse keeper fetish. But, seriously, are you on Grindr?"

When I started thumbing through Viv's issues of *Carter Exby Bulletin*, I realized that they were mixed in with a few issues of a Britpop fanzine called *slippery city*. When I eventually opened the first issue of *slippery city*, I saw that its table of contents was written in Viv's stylized handwriting.

I was astonished. I paged through it, looking for its writer's name. The only one I could find was *velocity girl* written in lowercase letters. The mailing address was a PO box in our city. I messaged Dot. Did Viv have a fanzine called slippery city?! An hour or so later, she replied with four spitfire texts:

Yes!

Do you have them??

At work now

Bring them over tonight

There appeared to be only three issues of *slippery city: the brit-pop fanzine*. I found the self-assuredness of subtitling it "the britpop fanzine" (rather than "a britpop fanzine") refreshing and amusing. It was a black-and-white stapled zine with a cut-and-paste DIY aesthetic. I scanned each issue's table of contents and, while most of the pieces revolved around Britpop, there were a few entries on nonmusical topics, including one on cycling, a few on old horror films, and one about silver (Viv's favourite colour).

The first issue included the following gloss on Viv's nom de plume (written in her handwriting):

> *if you wanna know why i'm called what i'm called*
> *it's because of primal scream's PERFECT little pop song*
> *with the perfect title → velocity girl*
> *but it's also because some girls are quicker than others*
> *some girls need to reach escape velocity*
> *to break through the atmosphere*
> *and i am one of those lightning quick girls*
> *i'm one of those velocity girls*

In the second issue, a reader named Roger complained that some of the music discussed in her zine didn't qualify as Britpop.

Viv's response was handwritten across a xeroxed image of barbed wire:

roger that roger dodger
well that's funny because i think any british music from the
80s and 90s is britpop
if you disagree that's fine but you're wrong
and you'll always be wrong
do you read me?
velocity girl over and out

After dinner, I biked through twenty minutes of drizzle and fog to Dot's apartment. When she let me in, she whispered that Teddy was already dozing. I gingerly took the three issues of *slippery city* out of my backpack and put them on the kitchen table. I saw Teddy stretched out on the couch. Dot smiled when she saw the zines.

"I have copies of these somewhere," she said quietly. "But I have no idea where they are. Maybe at our parents' house. If they come across them, I'm sure they'll throw them in the fireplace." She gritted her teeth.

"These are yours," I said. "I can scan copies for myself."

She nodded and turned her attention to the first issue.

While the articles in Viv's zine were largely about Britpop, they were also intensely personal. I saw Dot was looking at a piece on the Suede song "Animal Nitrate" that could have been subtitled "an ode to bottoming." It casually mentioned some of the drugs Viv had taken to enhance sex, including amyl nitrite. In it, she described herself as "basically the best bratty bottom ever." I wondered what it was like for Dot to read her sister's zine, especially because it was so sexual and unguarded.

"Did Viv talk to you about her zine?" I asked.

"She gave me copies of each issue," Dot said, "so she definitely wasn't hiding it."

"I could only find three issues. Do you remember how many she published?"

"Three. That was it. She was tired of paying for a PO box and she didn't want to include her address."

I wanted to ask Dot about Viv's life before I knew her, but I knew that if Viv had wanted me to know about it, she would have told me herself. It wasn't my place to probe into her past.

While I was putting on my coat and getting ready to leave, I noticed Dot was holding on to a wrapped gift. Teddy was near her, sleepily playing with a toy airplane.

"Uh, Dot," I said. "That better not be for me."

"Don't worry," she said. "It's really small. A tiny gift." She paused. "I know you don't want people to know when your birthday is. And I want to respect that, but Viv had it on her calendar and she would have done something. So I did something. I hope that's okay. I know it's a few days early, but I probably won't see you on the actual day."

I've always tended to keep my birthday to myself. Christopher and my parents know when it is. The only other people I've told have been girlfriends because they always ask. My friends have never really asked. Viv was my only friend who knew. She'd cajoled/charmed it out of me. I held out as long as I could.

"Look," I told Viv, "birthdays are like assholes. Everyone has them and most of them stink."

Viv shot me a look. "My asshole doesn't stink," she said.

"I didn't mean that," I said.

"Now you better tell me," she said, "or my asshole is gonna sulk all night."

So, I told her when my birthday was. She got me a small gift and made sure we toasted my birthday every year.

"Thanks," I said to Dot. She handed me the gift, and I looked down at the wrapping paper. It was adorned with cats in spacesuits. It was almost too adorable to unwrap.

"I just don't like people to make a fuss," I said. "Everybody has birthdays." I shrugged.

"I think you're worth making a fuss over," Dot said. "And so does Teddy."

I stooped down and asked Teddy to help me tear open the gift-wrap. Once I made a small tear in the paper, Teddy grabbed it and yanked. He was a whiz at tearing things. Last year, I'd given him a gorgeous children's book written by a trans writer. Dot had immediately scooped it out of Teddy's tiny hands and hid it on a bookshelf up high, saying, "I'll keep this book safe until he's able to turn the pages without ripping them."

Under the wrapping paper was a framed piece of art. Generally, giving me art is not a good idea. I'm picky, and most people have terrible taste in art. Dot has great taste. She might even have better taste than me. I held up the framed art. It looked like three paper dolls.

"I hope you like it," Dot said. "They're paper dolls that Zelda Fitzgerald made in the thirties or forties. It's the Big Bad Wolf from *Little Red Riding Hood*."

"These are phenomenal," I said. "I don't know what to say."

I looked more closely at the paper dolls. One doll showed the Big Bad Wolf in red lingerie. Another doll had the wolf in a white dress, holding a small bouquet of daisies. On the third doll, the wolf (this time without a face) wore a black cowl, black boots, and had an array of rifles and daggers.

"When I saw it in a little store on Main Street, I thought of you," she said.

"I love it. Thank you so much. And thank you, Teddy."

He looked at me.

"High five?" I asked, holding up my open palm. He looked away and left me hanging.

Dot shrugged. "Sometimes you get a high five," she said, "and sometimes you get a big zero."

I laughed.

"I love you. Now, go home. I've gotta put Teddy to bed before he gets cranky."

I hugged her goodbye. Teddy didn't feel like hugging right then. I tried again for a high five. He blinked and went back to playing with his toy airplane. When I was standing in the doorway, I waved theatrically at Teddy. He waved back. It was no high five, but it was something.

A few days later, a birthday card from my parents arrived in the mail. As usual, my mom signed it for herself and my dad. On my birthday, my mom called. An hour or so later, Christopher called. (I think my mom has to remind him every year.) Dot texted me a small video of herself and Teddy wishing me a happy birthday. For dinner, I got takeaway from an Indian-Chinese place nearby and picked up a pint of peanut butter chocolate chip ice cream. Whisk curled up alongside me on the couch. I took the night off from *Little Blue* and lost myself in a graphic novel about a queer young girl who's obsessed with monsters and horror films.

Pp

Herman PARK is a member of the garage rock band Teach Yourself Beekeeping, which also includes Sherman and Thurman Park. The Parks live together in a house with three front doors, one for each band member, making them almost seem like *The Monkees*. I was always confused about why they moved to Little Blue Island because it's not the ideal setting for an aspiring band. Herman is the band's lead singer and main lyricist. In case you can't make out what Herman is singing during their shambolic performance at Little Blue Pub, here it is:

Gimme little taste
Gimme little squeeze
Gimme little squirt …
Of your …
Electric juice!

Herman is one of the characters most associated with anti-quated forms of technology. We see him using a wind-up gramophone, and he sends a message via Morse code with an electrical telegraph. According to my sources, the Morse code message Herman sends is "Draw your sword and get ready."

Sherman PARK is the bee's knees. Sherman plays bass, works at a candy store called Sugar Glider, and is a dandy, favouring Italian suits and distinctive hats. It's not surprising that when Ian Earl Stairs wants advice on "getting dressed to impress a pretty lady," he goes to Sherman, who is undeniably the most stylish character on the island. Sadly, Ian quickly disproves Sherman's maxim that "you can never go wrong with a bespoke suit and a bow tie." During his awkward pur-suit of Ranjit Jha, Ian wears a tailored pumpkin-coloured suit and skull-and-crossbones-patterned bow tie.

Sherman is an openly trans-masculine character who is playful and irresistible at a time when trans characters rarely appeared in television or film without being ridiculed or attacked. Viv's femme poise owed something to Sherman's understated swagger.

Viv and I both loved Sherman and how free he seems to be in his body. Look at those uninhibited dance moves to Tommy Roe's "Jam Up and Jelly Tight" in the empty candy store. It's impossible to imagine another character on *Little Blue* moving so unselfconsciously in a public space.

As an aside, can we all agree that Tommy Roe's song "Jam Up and Jelly Tight" is catchy as hell, but sounds like the work of a sexual predator? How can every line in the song be so creepy? Who walks up to a woman and says he's going to pet her? And the title is about fucking her, right? The only saving grace is the line about her giving him permission, but even then it sounds like he's gonna try parlaying a single kiss into the whole shebang. Fuck you, Tommy Roe. Okay, forget the song. In this scene, Sherman dances with an I-belong-here-ness that's palpable. And the same sense pervades every one of his scenes in *Little Blue*.

Thurman PARK is the quietest member of Teach Yourself Beekeeping. He plays drums, he's dating Alison Kim, and he seems fond of backgammon. He must have come up with the band name because he's also an amateur beekeeper. When he suggests the band perform live in beekeeping suits, Sherman dismisses the idea. "What we really need," Sherman says, "is matching blazers covered in swarms of bees." Thurman never broaches the topic again.

Agnes PENNYPACKER, the island arborist, is another character Viv loved. Like many fans, she was inspired and moved by Agnes wearing medical supplies as fashion accessories. Agnes's introduction on the show isn't until the third episode, when she appears in the diner with her arm in a sling. In the following episode, the sling is gone and she's wearing a surgical mask. This puzzled most viewers because it wasn't explained. Her hearing aid in the fifth episode is when people really started to complain. In the sixth episode, we learn that Agnes accessorizes her outfits with these items to honour her deceased husband, Edgar, who operated a medical supply shop.

A catalogue of medical supplies worn by Agnes Penny-packer:

> Episode 3: arm sling (left arm)
> Episode 4: surgical mask
> Episode 5: hearing aid
> Episode 6: latex gloves (both hands)
> Episode 7: neck brace
> Episode 8: stethoscope
> Episode 9: surgical cap
> Episode 10: eye patch (right eye)

If you aren't obsessed with *Little Blue*, you may be unaware of Little Blue Ballyhoo, a weekend-long gathering of fans that happens every year on Cruikshank Island. There are tours of locations, conversations with people involved in the show, trivia contests, episode screenings, and character look-alike contests. The most popular look-alike characters are invariably Sherman Park and Agnes Pennypacker. I only tagged along with Viv at Little Blue Ballyhoo once, and it was a whirlwind weekend of fandom. Everywhere you turned there was someone with an encyclopedic knowledge of the show. (My apologies if any of you picked up this book hoping to learn something new. This book is more thin crust than deep dish.) The atmosphere during the Ballyhoo is charged and welcoming.

Viv entered the look-alike contest as Agnes. She looked stunning in her eye patch, even though she didn't win. There were at least five or six spot-on Agneses in the same room, which was dizzying to behold. Viv veered away from Agnes's typical white-silk-shirt-and-jeans aesthetic and chose to rock an arbutus-print tunic and leggings, which may have been off-putting to some of the judges. But how can you deduct points for creativity? Shouldn't a higher difficulty level be taken into consideration like in the Olympics? Agnes is an arborist for goodness' sake. And she had to wear an eye patch after that raccoon leaped at her from an arbutus tree while she was surveying trees in Chappy Park. Shrug.

Viv always dressed for Halloween. Her go-to costumes were Agnes Pennypacker and the Bride of Frankenstein. Very few people are familiar with *Little Blue*, so she would always get more attention as the Bride of Frankenstein. Plus, prominently displaying her tattoo of the Bride's profile didn't hurt. She would stay in character the entire night—wide-eyed, moving awkwardly, silent—to a degree that people around her (even me, but especially her lovers) found maddening.

Edgar PENNYPACKER ran a medical supply shop for over twenty years and died under mysterious circumstances. While narrating the baseball game, Tindra North reveals that Edgar founded the Little Blue Cubs baseball team shortly after moving with Agnes to the island. She also explains that he was an amateur vexillographer and designed the island's elegant flag. Jenny Pennypacker's ability to catch breaking balls thrown by Mr. Bits is partly a result of coaching from her father, who Tindra says had been a "gifted catcher."

In every episode of *Little Blue*, we see characters who are still grieving the loss of their loved ones who have died or disappeared. Ranjit Jha misses Captain Alphonse and tells their son about how handsome and kind his father was. Emmanuel Curwood keeps a diary addressed to his dead twin sister Emma, and Stephanie Marberry's grief for her deceased best friend is palpable in every one of her scenes. Not only does Roy Spittle remind his daughter daily how much her mom Ivy loved her and how bright and creative she was ("She wasn't a princess in a castle, Paulie," he says while tucking her in. "She was better than a princess. She made a castle. She made a castle!"), all of Roy's paintings after she died are dedicated to her. While Agnes Pennypacker wears her husband Edgar's remaining medical supplies to remember him, her daughter Jenny secretly constructs a diorama of the 1893 world's fair in Chicago to commemorate her father, who we learn was obsessed with the fair his entire life.

We also have Mitch Marberry, whose parents we know will soon be killed, playing Banquo's ghost in *Macbeth*. It's particularly poignant when Banquo's ghost disappears and Emmanuel Curwood in the role of Macbeth raises a toast to Banquo, who he has just had murdered: "And to our dear friend Banquo, whom we miss; / Would he were here!" In nearly every scene of *Little Blue*, we have one or more characters who are communicating through words or actions that they still miss their loved ones and wish they were here. It's hard to think of a more fitting toast than raising a glass to the people we still love who are no longer with us.

Jenny PENNYPACKER, Agnes and Edgar's daughter, works at the post office and is engaged to Chet Tully, though she threatens to call off the wedding if he can't control his growing obsession with pigeon racing. An experienced spelunker, Jenny takes Delia and Ren Crease into the caves on the island, where they encounter a colony of bats.

The opening credit sequences for *Little Blue* are easily the most intricate ones I've seen. My favourite opening sequence is the one set to "Magnificent Obsession" by Lambchop. It shows dozens of characters indulging in their obsessions. Derek Hands guzzling coffee. Chet Tully feeding his racing pigeons. Jenny Pennypacker constructing her secret diorama. "Half Bloomer" Ambleside folding an origami duck. Each character is shown with their obsession for a second. Then, the frame freezes and the screen goes black except for the actor's silhouette, which becomes a single, bright colour. According to Eric Minor, this particular opening sequence was inspired by the opening credits for the corny music sitcom *The Partridge Family*. Derek's silhouette becomes mustard yellow. Chet turns turquoise. Jenny is dark red. "Half Bloomer" is mauve. Each character has a different colour. Seeing characters indulging in their obsessions always makes me somewhat jealous. I've never had that one thing that fascinates me, whether it's fishing or baseball or travelling or natural history. Maybe I'm wrong, but it seems like it would be comforting to have a particular fixation, something that shrinks the world into one little thing you can focus on through the telescope of your obsession.

Viv's favourite sequence was the one that uses Suede's song "Sleeping Pills." It shows each character going to bed and has several clips in slow motion, making a handful of characters look tranquilized. Even though Eric Minor claimed not to love *Little Blue,* he was generally enthralled by its opening sequences. He was always quick to point out how Tina Veverka had worked some editing magic to elevate a moment. Sometimes it was split-screens; sometimes it was jump-cuts; sometimes it was colour filters. He kept likening her to a magician who could conjure anything she wanted with the footage she was given.

Viv was partial to pills, including sleeping pills. When we were out, she would sometimes pop a pill or two in her mouth, tilt her head back and swallow it with a sip of something or other. Sometimes they were femme pills. Other times they weren't. When I'd ask her what she was taking, she'd typically say, "Don't worry about it." I knew she'd dabbled in a variety of substances. I'd seen her pie-eyed more than once, but I'm the kind of person who has no idea if someone is on MDMA or cocaine or just didn't get enough sleep last night. Once, a guy Viv was dating offered me a bump of coke. Viv laughed so hard when it happened. She said I didn't need anything, that I was a "good girl." Then she smooshed his cheeks with one of her hands and kissed him. Normally, I loved it when she called me a good girl, but this time it stung. I'd heard from a mutual friend who I trusted that Viv had said unkind things about me more than once. I was an art snob; I was pretentious; I was a cuddle slut. These things were all true, but I didn't like her describing me to strangers as a killjoy goody two-shoes.

When I was thirteen, I had a small circle of friends. One of us lived near the school, and sometimes we would hang out at his house at lunch time. While we were all walking to his place one day, Danny sidled up to me.

"Where are you going?" he asked me.

"Uh, I thought we were going to your house," I said.

He shook his head. "I didn't invite you. I don't want you in my house."

I felt sick and embarrassed and angry. I glanced over at my other friends. They were talking about something and hadn't noticed. Danny was watching me. "Okay," I murmured. I turned around and started walking back to the school. I wanted to punch myself in the face. I kept walking.

Later, when my friend Sam asked why I hadn't been with them at lunch, I told him what Danny had said. He said that he would have stood up for me, that he wouldn't have gone to Danny's place without me. The next day, Danny surprised me by inviting me to his house for lunch. I asked if he was sure he wanted me to come, and he said that he did. I didn't ask him why he'd disembowelled me the day before. I hated myself for not rejecting his offer to go to his house that day, but I needed friends, even if I couldn't always trust them.

I never asked Viv if she gossiped about me because I never wanted to confirm that she secretly snickered about me with her other, cooler friends. If I didn't ask her, maybe it wasn't true. I think I needed Viv more than she needed me, just like I had needed Danny. It would be lovely if relationships were immune to power dynamics, but they aren't.

Louise QUINCE is Leora Blest's lover. She is in the background of several scenes in the diner and at the Little Blue Soda Company, where she works in the bottling plant. Louise is best known for appearing in the most controversial scene in *Little Blue*. It starts off as a tender, playful scene with Louise and Leora talking and kissing at the kitchen table before segueing into a brief sequence with strobe-like editing that suggests a few sexual acts that most mainstream audiences had never seen on film before, including what appears to be Louise fisting Leora, though it's impossible to tell from the angle we see. Even though Vivian wasn't queer, she prized

Little Blue's bravery in showing queer sex. And this sequence runs the gamut of queer sex, managing to suggest everything from cunnilingus to using a strap-on to fisting in six seconds of screen time. It always cheers me up to see this blink-and-you'll-miss-it sequence. Louise and Leora both look sweaty and happy. I can't help feeling giddy when I see happy, sexy queers.

Among the outtakes on the *Little Blue* DVD box set put out by Ambidextrous Editions (or, as its pretentious logo has it, æmbidextrous ǝditions) is a brief scene of Louise crying while ironing a skirt. The context is unclear, but it looks cool when her tears sizzle as they land on the iron's hot underbelly, which the internet says I should call a "sole plate." While Louise irons and weeps, the radio plays the song "I Know You" by the Dave Clark Five, suggesting that maybe her relationship with Leora is more turbulent than we are otherwise shown.

The first time I went to Viv's apartment, I saw she had a framed black-and-white photograph on her bedroom wall of two women kissing. One of them was in a wheelchair. At first, I thought the photo meant Viv was queer. When I asked about the image, she left the room and returned a minute later with a copy of Suede's first album. On its cover was a cropped close-up of the same two women kissing. When their faces were all you saw, they looked like androgynous lovers.

"Do you know Suede?" Viv asked. I shook my head. She opened her mouth and her eyes so widely that she looked like a cartoon character. I started laughing.

"You will hear Suede. You MUST hear Suede. But, first," she said, "I'll make us cocktails."

I followed her into the kitchen. She made us a couple

of bourbon sours. She handed me mine and it was bracingly sour. She always made them extra sour. Sometimes when she ordered them in bars, she'd ask for hers to be "super fucking tart," playfully adding, "just like me."

Before she dropped the needle on the album's first song, she made me promise to listen and not judge. She even got me to repeat that phrase back to her: "listen and not judge."

Then, she introduced me to Suede. The first song was called "So Young." It sounded like seventies-era Bowie, when he was at his queerest. It was dramatic and theatrical. At first, I couldn't make out what the singer was singing. The parts that I understood were about being young and chasing a dragon. Halfway through the song, Viv couldn't resist grabbing a remote control from the coffee table as a microphone and lip-synching along with the singer. Her shiny red top showed a little cleavage. I had to concentrate on not making too much eye contact or looking too closely at her body as she writhed in front of me. It was so hot. I sipped my bourbon sour and tried not to visualize her hands against my throat while she fucked me. Then, the song slowed its tempo and stopped.

She collapsed beside me on the couch and leaned over to place the remote control on the coffee table. I kept sneaking little looks at her and tried to relax and listen to Suede. After a few songs, my glass was empty, but I kept tilting it, getting a small taste of the lingering egg-white foam each time.

When side A ended, she turned to me with bright eyes. "Should I make us more bourbon sours and play side B?"

"Yes, please!"

She went and made another batch. They didn't seem quite as sour this time, but I think it's because I was getting slightly tipsy and my tastes were already sliding towards what Viv liked. She walked over to the turntable and flipped the album. The first song was overwrought and sensual and awash in drama. Most of the lines that popped out at me were about sex and drugs and death. I kept stealing glances of Viv as she drank her bourbon sour. After each sip, she would unconsciously lick the froth from her lips. The first song on this side ended with the line "You're taking me over, oooh" repeated again and again. It was hypnotic.

When the last song on the album faded, she turned to me expectantly. "So?" she asked. "Have I turned you into a Suedehead?"

"A what?" I laughed.

"A Suedehead, babe," she said. "A Suedehead. You will be one. Eventually. Trust me."

Her phone pinged. She checked it. "Oh!" she said. "Gotta go, babe. Time to get fucked."

"Okay, cool," I said. "That was fun."

"It's hard to go wrong with cocktails and Suede," she said.

After a quick hug, I hurried out the door only to wend my way back to my tiny apartment.

Rr

RINGO is Chet Tully's prize racing pigeon. Chet hides Ringo in the trunk of his car after promising his fiancée, Jenny Pennypacker, that he will sell his pigeons to another enthusiast. Shortly thereafter, he reveals to Timmy Whiffle that Ringo will be the secret ring bearer when he marries Jenny.

Ringo the Pigeon was a pretty talented animal actor. He could coo up a storm. Viv once got into an argument about pigeons with her friend Tessa while we were walking along the seawall. Tessa hated pigeons, calling them "rats with wings." Viv brought up their cute-ass coo. Tessa didn't budge on her distaste for them. I mentioned that they were also called rock doves. "Now, rock doves sound cute, right, Tess?" Viv asked. Tessa shook her head.

This summer, an artist turned parts of the route for our rapid-transit train into a Disney-like ride. One tunnel became a cave with stalactites, stalagmites, and a colony of animatronic bats with glowing pink eyes. Another spot along the route had an enormous abominable snowman looming above the train, looking down at us with oversized anime-style eyes. A few months after I gave her Viv's shoes and boots, Tessa invited me to lunch at a hip new Korean restaurant that specialized in beer and chicken. We took transit to the restaurant, which was in a nondescript suburban strip mall. Somehow, Tessa hadn't heard anything about the art installation along the route. She lost it when bats with hot-pink eyes flew by her train window when we entered the tunnel. I told her everything was okay, that this was an art project that the city had approved. She didn't believe me at first, but I persuaded her by pointing to articles about the project on my phone. To my surprise, she was delighted when the massive abominable snowman suddenly appeared, raising its arms in the air and staring down at us.

At the restaurant, we shared a pitcher of cold beer and an order of fried chicken with green onions. Tessa was still stunned by the art she'd whipped past on the train. When she calmed down she asked if it was true that I was writing a book about Vivian. I had only told a few people about the book project. I told her that, yes, I was writing a book about Viv, but that I wasn't sure that I even wanted to publish it, which was true. She had a lot of follow-up questions. What was in the book? Who was mentioned? Was she mentioned?

Why did I need to write it? What made me an expert on Viv? Was I capitalizing on the death of my friend?

"You didn't know her that well," she said at one point.

"There's a lot about her that I don't know," I said. "I'm just trying to preserve some of my memories before they vanish. Viv wasn't a saint, but her life mattered to me. And to lots of other people. What didn't I know about her?"

Tessa just smirked and sipped her beer.

I didn't want to answer any of her questions. I didn't want to justify writing about Viv. I didn't want to be stuck in a Korean chicken and beer joint with her. I asked for the cheque. When it arrived, I told Tessa I'd get it. She nodded without looking up from her phone. Day drinking was not her friend. I pointed to the train station that would take her back downtown. She glowered at me.

As I stood up at the table, I noticed that Tessa was wearing Viv's blue Fluevogs. Viv was always on the hunt for spectacular shoes in her size. She scoured thrift stores regularly and had her feelers out via friends who knew to text her when they spotted a promising-looking pair of size tens. She'd been so elated the day she found those cobalt-blue ankle boots. And now Tessa was wearing them while telling me that I was capitalizing on my friendship with Viv. That Wicked Witch of the West didn't deserve Viv's fabulous blue Fluevogs.

I said goodbye to Tessa and left the restaurant, walking through the mall parking lot. My fingers were shaking as I fitted the earbuds into my ears. I hit PLAY on my phone. It was Ringo Starr's "I'm the Greatest." I smiled. It was the perfect song for that imperfect moment. It made me think of Chet Tully's pigeon. It made me think of how Viv dismissed the Beatles with the phrase "beep beep, beep beep, yeah." But "all I wanna do is boogaloo" in "I'm the Greatest" was just as ludicrous. Suddenly, I wanted to be at karaoke surrounded by a handful of tipsy trans women, belting out "I'm the Greatest." I'd have to change a few words to make it work, but that would be easy peasy. And hearing a trans woman sing "I'm the Greatest" would be the greatest.

S s

Roy SPITTLE, his daughter Pauline Elder, and their dog Visconti are the first residents of Little Blue Island that Delia and Ren Crease encounter. Roy runs the island's RV park, which was designed by his late wife, Ivy Elder. Roy's abstract paintings belong in the same abstract colour field painting style as Beulah Holmstrom's work *Red No. 42*, which Viv and I encountered together in the art gallery and prompted her to bring me into the *Little Blue* fold. As you'd expect, his current indigo, violet, and yellow canvases based on Ivy's name are much darker than were the red, orange, and yellow canvases based on his own name.

" ROY: I still dream about Ivy nearly every night. Even last night. I was sitting in a dentist's chair. Looking around nervously at the equipment. Fidgeting. Waiting. Ivy walks in, starts unbuttoning my shirt.
DALTON: Whoa, whoa. Okay, stop.
ROY: Then she puts a stethoscope right here, above my heart. I can see a teardrop forming in the corner of her eye. She looks at me, tells me I'm not breathing. She says, "The passage is blocked." She reaches into her white coat and takes out a pair of pliers.
DALTON: Pliers?
ROY: Yeah, pliers. She tells me to relax, that her only option is to remove my teeth so I can breathe again.
DALTON: And?
ROY: And that's it. I wake up. And Visconti is on the bed, whimpering, looking at me. Because I'm weeping. **"**

I often dream of Viv. Sometimes I wake up in tears. In my dreams, she's sadder than the woman I knew. And most of the time she can't see or hear me, no matter how much I try to reach her. Like Roy, I once had a disturbing dream about her that involved teeth. I don't recall the context, but she suddenly turned to me and asked why I'd never brushed my inner teeth. I looked in the mirror and noticed that I had a second row of tiny teeth in my mouth tucked behind my regular teeth that I'd never noticed before. They had never been brushed and were black and rotting. Viv gave me a disgusted look and I awoke as a wave of shame washed over me.

Ian Earl STAIRS is the island's jittery, socially inept barber. His barbershop was previously owned by his father, who had rows of teeth strung across the window of the shop and several jars filled with pig's blood and leeches floating in formaldehyde. Ian replaced these with painted illustrations on the front window of teeth and leeches. The store's motto is "We cut heads."

"

IAN: Do you want any bad blood drained while you're sitting in my chair?
REN: Pardon?
IAN: Until the early nineteenth century, my brood—that is, the brood of barbers—performed a variety of tasks besides haircuts. We used to be barber-surgeons. I'm skilled at removing bad teeth and bad blood.
REN: Oh.
IAN: I haven't lost a patient yet! Ha!

"

Ian's misguided courtship of Ranjit Jha exemplifies Isobel Lacroix's characterization of him as "creepy but mostly harmless." ("Mostly harmless" may be overly generous because it's unclear what Ian intends to do with the shipment of jimsonweed he receives. Jimsonweed can cause poisoning and death, though it's never revealed whether he plans to use it as a poison or a recreational intoxicant.) When Ranjit gently declines his attempts to woo her, Ian brings her a cassette labelled *1,000 Dances!* We hear thirty-five seconds of him singing an a cappella version of "Nobody but Me" with a laundry list of invented dances.

"

No no, no, no no, no no no no
No no, no, no no, no no no no, no no, no no no

Nobody can do the Turkey Beak like I do!
Nobody can do the Wiggle Room like I do!
Nobody can do the Flugelhorn like I do!
Nobody can do the Salad Fork like I do! **"**

Ian Earl Stairs is played by Bruce McCulloch, best known for being a member of the Canadian sketch comedy troupe *The Kids in the Hall*. It's worth noting that he later released the original twenty-four-minute-long version of "Nobody but Me" (with all 1,000 invented dances!) on his website: www.brucio.com. Unfortunately, it appears to be temporarily unavailable.

Viv couldn't really sing, but I still think she would have been a captivating front person for a band. After we watched the magical Swedish film *We Are the Best!* about three teenage girls starting a punk band in the early eighties, I was keen to start a band composed of all trans women. Viv was less enthusiastic, but she indulged me. She even came up with the name Phantom Womb, which would have fit a band of trans femmes like a haute couture dress. Viv would be the singer. I played piano as a kid and could probably play keyboard well enough to write some punk songs. My friend Trina said she could play guitar or bass, whichever one we needed, as long as she didn't have to pay for the rehearsal space. I asked all the trans women I knew if any of them could play drums. They couldn't. One night, I got a text from someone I knew from a support group that I used to attend. She said that she'd seen the profile for a cute trans girl on a dating site who answered the question, What are you good at? by writing I'm decent at drumming and I'm great at bottoming! :) It was free to join the dating site, so I did. I messaged her. I waited. She never wrote me back. After a few weeks, I gave up on my dream of playing keyboard in a band with Viv.

I'd nearly forgotten about Phantom Womb until Ruby told me about an upcoming show at a small club by a band of trans women. By the time the show happened, Ruby had phased me out of her life. She had gone to Portland for a couple of weeks with her girlfriend Robin. When she returned, she would wait days to return my texts and, even then, would only send brief, vague replies. I eventually understood that she didn't want to date me anymore. Message received. Or, more accurately, message not received. It had been that kind of week. I was supposed to go with Ruby, but I texted Nora to see if she wanted to see Femme Task Force with me. Less than a minute later, she replied, FUCK YES!!!

The club was crammed with even more queer and trans femmes than I'd expected. Femme Task Force had attitude for days, along with an incredible aesthetic—especially the guitarist, in her sequined red bra and matching lipstick, glittery nails, and six-inch candy-apple-red platform heels. They were sloppy and there seemed to be some tension in the band, particularly between the singer and the bassist. They hadn't been around long, but they had already put out a ferocious EP called *We Have an Agenda*. They were inspiring and breathtaking live.

They ended the night with a fiery performance of their song "Give the Trans Girl Some." When they moved into the chorus, I almost levitated. The singer Evie sang, "Give the trans girl some! Some what?" And the audience roared back, "Some love!" I was in the thick of things, roaring with a crowd of queer and trans femmes and smiling at Nora, who had one of her arms around my waist, and I felt seen and desired, and most of my sadness at being rejected by Ruby melted away. They repeated the chorus a few extra times, the room getting louder and louder.

> *Give the trans girl some!*
> *Some what?*
> *SOME LOVE!*

> *Give the trans girl some!*
> *Some what?*
> *SOME LOVE!!!*

> *Give the trans girl some!*
> *Some what?*
> *SOME LOVE!!!!!!!*

Then, the band pushed into the song's final refrain:

> *Give the trans girls some!*
> *Some love!*
> *Some love!*
> *Some LUH-UH-UH-UH-UV!!*

Most of us were already singing along, but Evie yelled that she needed to hear everybody. The crowd got louder than ever and our desire for love and sex was almost palpable, especially during the undulating final word.

> *Give the trans girls some!*
> *Some love!*
> *Some love!*
> *Some LUH-UH-UH-UH-UV!!*

> *Give the TRANS GIRLS SOME!*

Some LOVE!
Some LOVE!
Some LUH-UH-UH-UH-UV!!!

GIVE THE TRANS GIRLS SOME!!
SOME LOVE!!
SOME LOVE!!
SOME LUH-UH-UH-UH-UV!!!!!

The din stopped on a dime. A couple of women in the band waved theatrical goodbyes before exiting the stage. The lights grew brighter and I was surrounded by dozens of exhilarated, lustful femmes. Oh, how I needed that show that night.

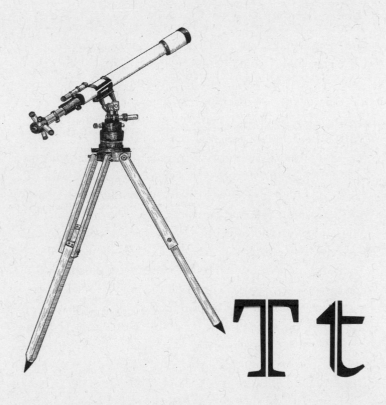

T t

Toshiro TANAKE was one of the earliest settlers on Little Blue Island. He was renowned for his delicious and abundant cucumber crops. In 1942, the Japanese families located on the island were evacuated to internment camps. Shortly thereafter, the government confiscated their land and possessions to finánce their internment and to pressure them to resettle elsewhere. Charles "Chappy." Ambleside purchased Tanake's land and adopted his wildly successful cultivation techniques. Chappy's son, Roderick Ambleside, confesses to Stephen Marberry that Toshiro Tanake appeared in one of his dreams, pelting him with tomatoes and cucumbers. Then, via dream logic, Roderick found himself transported into a carnival dunk tank with a crowd of Japanese Canadians throwing baseballs and insults at him as he pleaded for them to stop.

One of my recurring nightmares is that there will be a devastating earthquake. When I was a kid, we were told that a massive earthquake could hit our part of the world at any time, and definitely within our lifetimes. We watched videos in class about tectonic plates and the destructive powers of earthquakes. During earthquake drills, we would scoot under our desks and point our bums towards the windows, cupping our necks with our little hands. It's no wonder that I have vivid nightmares. Or, actually, I dream about the aftermath of earthquakes. My tree-covered city has shifted into a desert with piles of rubble here and there. Everyone is wearing leather pants and driving souped-up muscle cars, carrying clubs with spikes. Okay, fine, I basically dream about a *Mad Max*–style post-apocalyptic wasteland. I don't normally see any zombies, but there's always the sense that they could stumble into the scene.

I was always too embarrassed to tell Viv about my post-apocalyptic nightmares, but I think she would have understood that my two dominant fears in these nightmares were whether my loved ones were okay and whether I had access to a stockpile of hormones. In my dreams, drugstores are places where I always run into a straggle of bruisers. They're there for their drugs; I'm there for my drugs. They think I want their drugs; I know they don't want my drugs. Sometimes I have a crowbar, sometimes I have a slotted spoon. I normally fail to get my drugs, but on those rare occasions when I do succeed, I am jubilant.

When we were dating, Ruby talked me into watching a zombie movie with her one night. I tend to avoid anything

with zombies in it because I don't enjoy watching loboto-
mized undead creatures lumber around trying to kill people
and chew on their brains. Not my cuppa. Somehow, Ruby
persuaded me. It was a Taiwanese film, and Ruby's family
is from Taiwan. Plus, it was about cute zombie cats. I was
intrigued. Until the first clutch of cats started eating the
brains of a kindly shopkeeper. One moment he's petting the
cats and scratching behind their ears. A second later, a huge
tomcat leaps down from above and slams the shopkeeper's
skull against the floor. Crack. The tomcat has glowing red
eyes. This was not the film I was hoping to watch. Even
Ruby was taken aback. Thankfully, making out is a good way
to wipe out images of cat carnage.

Chet TULLY is a baker and a pigeon racer. He delivers
his Chet the Baker baked goods to stores in the sidecar of
his Vespa scooter. He is engaged to Jenny Pennypacker and
sports a handlebar moustache.

" JENNY: Are you hungry?
CHET: I was born hungry!

ROLAND: Are you serious?
CHET: I was born serious!

TIMMY: Are you shitting me?
CHET: I was born shitting you! "

I was always baffled by how Jenny Pennypacker could be
attracted to Chet's blustery masculinity. But Viv was confused
by my confusion. She found it cute that he overcompensated

for riding a scooter by referring to it as his "mighty steed."
She was also charmed by how worried Chet gets about
losing his "mojo." Is that code for his masculinity? When I
transitioned, I let the uncomfortable shell of masculinity I'd
been shouldering dissolve. Masculinity had always felt corro-
sive and constrictive. It was an oily toxin I was expected to
drench myself in. Viv tried explaining to me how intoxicat-
ing masculinity could be, but I never understood. If I see a
few masculine dudes taking up space together, I tend to drift
away from them. I've taken to thinking of these congrega-
tions of men as murders of bros.

I've been writing this encyclopedia on Vivian's laptop. After
several days of writing, my curiosity finally got the better
of me, and I opened a folder on the desktop called "beautiful
pain." It contained a slew of photos of Viv's body covered in
bruises and welts and cuts. A few of them also showed her face.
She looked satisfied. She looked content. She looked trium-
phant. I hadn't wanted to hear about the darker parts of her
life, so she'd kept them from me. At the time, I didn't realize
she was doing what she needed to do. She decided how she
would be hurt and when and by whom. She choreographed
her pain. Her body was hers. She could do what she wanted
with it. I still wrestle with even acknowledging my own darkness to myself, let alone triumphing over it.

Beside me on the desk, I had a to-do list on a sticky note.
I added an item to the list: *Turn pain into beauty*. It seemed
as elusive as turning lead into gold, but somehow Viv had
done it. And I suppose that I've been trying to perform a
similar emotional alchemy by turning the pain of losing Viv
into a weepy and witty alphabetical elegy. So far, it hasn't
really made me feel alphabetter, but it has made me realize

Ranjit Jha was right when she talked about her absent husband Captain Alphonse, saying, "we love the dog we love, dirt and all." Sometimes we realize too late that we didn't appreciate the dirt and the darkness.

May UNDERWOOD works at Grady Goodwin's drive-in theatre. She breaks up with Tycho Brahe to go back to her on-again, off-again boyfriend Timmy Whiffle. Tycho names a comet after May, and she returns to him. In the final minutes of the last episode, May drops a bombshell by confiding to Alison Kim that she is pregnant, though she doesn't disclose whether the father is Tycho or Timmy. It has to be Tycho. It has to be Tycho. It has to be Tycho.

May slays with her femme style. She's a burst of cuteness in her array of polka-dot dresses, high heels, and blood-red lipstick. Many people see May as a caricature of femininity, but she's clearly more nuanced. She owns her femmeness and speaks her mind. No other character would be as open as she is about her reason for returning to an old lover: "He knows how to fuck me." Timmy Whiffle? Her honesty is refreshing, but ick. Plus, she's the only character who says the word "cunt." And she says it repeatedly, my favourite time being her response to Timmy's confession that he's considering legally changing his name to Ace: "You're a cunt, Ace." At least she recognizes he's a fool, even if he's a fool who knows how she needs to be fucked. And people seem to forget that May hits the only home run in the Little Blue Bears versus Little Blue Cubs baseball game. (During the game, May wears tiny telescope earrings that can be glimpsed just before she hits her home run, a subtle signal that she still cares for Tycho. It has to be Tycho's baby. It has to be.)

Obviously, Viv loved May. Viv had two amazing polka-dot dresses, as well as a polka-dot winter coat. Dot later told me how Viv would entertain Teddy by alternating pointing at the dots on her dress and at Dot, saying the word "dot" again and again until Teddy was awash in giggles.

I recently went to an installation called *Defeated Umbrellas* that Viv would have loved. The entire second floor of the art gallery was covered in broken, abandoned umbrellas. Thousands and thousands of abandoned umbrellas. In several places, umbrellas were arranged in heaps that were taller than me. When you entered, the lights were dim and the umbrellas were all black. As you walked along a winding path, the umbrellas gradually shifted colour, becoming lighter and brighter, until you found yourself in an expanse of damaged, dazzling red umbrellas .

With my store discount, I once bought Viv an umbrella

with a cherry blossom design. When Dot and I were cleaning out her apartment, we found the umbrella. It had a couple of broken ribs and I wondered if this was the umbrella she'd held above a lover during a torrential downpour on a park bench one night. The rain fell in sheets while she held the umbrella and her lover fucked her in the darkness. She told me the umbrella she was holding had been damaged by the wind. She didn't talk about most of the sex she was having, but she couldn't resist this time. "I got so fucking wet," she said. "You have no idea. Drenched as fuck. Fucked as fuck. It was incredible!"

Now I wish Viv had told me which park bench along the seawall she'd been on that night. Maybe I could raise money to buy a plaque for it. *In loving memory of Vivian Cloze, who experienced one of the best fucks of her life during a rainstorm on this bench. She is missed.*

Vv

Jesse Garon VINGAARD is Roderick Ambleside's helicopter pilot. His face remains obscured throughout the series and his only line is "Roger that, Daddy." In *Carter Exby Bulletin*, Lucy Six wrote an astounding piece on the role of dead twins throughout *Little Blue*. For example, she traces the character Jesse Garon Vingaard's name to Jesse Garon Presley, who was Elvis Presley's stillborn twin brother, and Mads Vingaard, who owned a press in Copenhagen that Tycho Brahe used to publish a broadside about his stillborn twin brother in 1572. Lucy also reminds fans that the entire series is bookended with Emmanuel Curwood's diary entries to his dead twin sister, Emma. The first words we hear are "Dear Em, I didn't kill anyone, but people died," and the final words of the last episode are "I miss you so bloody much, Em."

VISCONTI is the three-legged beagle owned by Roy Spittle and his daughter, Pauline Elder. With a majestic name like Visconti, you would expect him to be a noble beagle, but in every scene he crackles with goofy energy, his tail swishing and his tongue hanging out. When I first heard the name Visconti on *Little Blue*, I pictured Italian film director Count Luchino Visconti and record producer Tony Visconti, most famous for his work in the seventies with David Bowie and T. Rex. I laughed when I realized Visconti was the name of the excitable dog licking Pauline Elder's face.

Viv loved cats, but she loved dogs even more. She wanted a dog so badly, but her building didn't allow pets. She lived near a dog park and often talked friends or lovers into going there with her. I always feel slightly uncomfortable in dog parks, sort of like an adult without kids sitting in a playground. Viv knew many of the dogs' names at the park and chatted easily with their owners, while I stood silently next to her. Viv also seemed to crush more easily on guys with cute dogs. She kept dating one or two awful guys much longer than she should have because she didn't want to stop seeing their dogs.

I can't bring myself to delete Viv's entry from my phone's list of contacts. "Vivian!" is still my only entry under the letter V. She'd added the exclamation mark to her name at the same time she wrote in the Notes section "VIVIAN RULES OK," followed by a red heart and a yellow heart. The small photo of her is one she sent me in the middle of the night. Her hair is dishevelled and she's puckering her bright red lips. She looks really drunk, but also really happy.

One of her last texts to me was i'm so broke babe. She wasn't sure she could cover her half of the rent. Her boyfriend at the time had borrowed some money and was ghosting her. I transferred her a few hundred dollars.

When I looked at that text from her just now, I initially thought it was i'm so broken babe. The last time I saw her, she was anything but broken. We met for brunch and she was still elated from dancing to dark eighties music the night before.

"The DJ was super fucking cute," she said. "But he was a stickler for the eighties thing. So, no Suede. I mean, fuck me. He played 'Sex Dwarf' like three fucking times. C'mon! That's too much 'Sex Dwarf,' babe."

"Got it," I said. "Two sex dwarfs is enough." I didn't know what she was talking about, but it sounded like a song. "Maybe that would be a good name for a film," I said. "The script would write itself. All you need is a star. Wait. I can see the posters now: 'Peter Dinklage is *Sex Dwarf*.'"

"Oh, wow," she said, laughing. "You really went with it. I know guys aren't your thing, but let me tell you: he's hot. I definitely wouldn't say no to a little Dinklage." She winked and sipped her mimosa. "Oh," she added. "I already said the DJ was cute, right?"

"You did," I said. "Super fucking cute."

"So cute!" Viv said. "He didn't play any Suede, but he played Morrissey's 'Suedehead' for me and he smiled his ass off when I sang along with the line 'It was a good lay, a good lay oh.' It was a pretty fucking good night." She couldn't resist adding, "I said it was a good lay, a good lay. Oh, such a good lay, a good lay."

I laughed.

Looking back at our old text messages on my phone, I

wanted so badly to text Viv, even if she couldn't reply. I typed I miss you so bloody much, Viv and sent it. I waited for the message to be delivered.

Ww

Timmy WHIFFLE is May Underwood's on-again, off-again weaselly boyfriend. He works at Little Blue General Store, where he also seems to be an indiscreet bookie specializing in pigeon racing. We see him apply for a job at the bottling plant, which may be a ploy to discover and profit from its secret "overcarbonation process." Timmy isn't entirely smarmy, as we learn when he volunteers to prove his love for May by defusing the unearthed bomb. The gesture is strangely touching, even though May isn't in danger and the bomb is soon revealed to be a movie prop.

> TIMMY: "Mediocre" always sounds like a way you could order your eggs in a restaurant. I'll get the Little Cowpoke breakfast with coffee.
> MAY: And how would you like your eggs done?
> TIMMY: Mediocre.
> MAY: With a side of milquetoast?
> TIMMY: Milk toast? You mean like French toast?
> MAY: Oh, Ace.

Part of the genius of *Little Blue* is that it funnels so much of the world around you into a single show, to such an extent that you can't help but be reminded of the series on a daily basis. When I spy a goofy name for a breakfast dish or order French toast, I often think of this scene.

WHOMPY is the ventriloquist's dummy that Roland Gorse passes down to his son, Freddy. At the school talent show, Whompy criticizes the judges and the other contestants. After Roland and Freddy lose the ability to speak, Whompy becomes surprisingly tender.

Over a dozen robins just landed in the English holly tree beside my bedroom window. They are really going to town, quickly plucking its bright red berries one by one with their beaks and swallowing them whole. Occasionally, they have to flutter their wings to steady themselves on the branches.

The first time Viv visited my apartment, I gave her a quick tour. In my room, I pulled up my venetian blinds so she could see the charming holly tree. One of the main reasons I like my apartment is my view of that holly tree. It gives me privacy and I adore its shiny dark green leaves with their creamy edges. I know it's an invasive species, but it's so gorgeous. And I especially love when birds land on it and start chirping and cheeping.

I tried to get Viv to go birding with me a few times, but she said it wasn't for her. Now that Viv is gone and I've steeped myself in the music she loved, I know that I might have convinced her to go birding by casually mentioning that Suede's first single was "The Drowners," which included "To the Birds" on its flip side. She would have been speechless that I'd delved into Suede. But I also knew she was right: birding wouldn't have been for her.

I texted Christopher to see if he wanted to go birding with me on the weekend. He replied with two bird emojis, followed by an index and pinky finger devil horns emoji. Rock out with your flock out, Chris.

My brother is the person who got me into paying attention to birds. They are one of his favourite things to draw. He bought me my first field guide and tried to get me to recognize a particular bird's details. I always had trouble telling species apart. Sure, I could spot a male red-winged blackbird with its unmissable red and yellow wing patch against its black feathers, but the female just looked like any other unremarkable dusty-brown bird. There were no red wings or black feathers on the females. When Chris would point out five different species of ducks in front of us, I'd do my best to notice all the differences, but there were just too many variations. I loved watching birds, but I was never going to be able to tell them all apart.

He drove us to a bird sanctuary and we bought two types of birdseed, one for ducks and one for chickadees. They told us there were two types of owls in the trees along the East Dyke Trail.

"What do you say, Chris? Make a beeline for the East Dyke?" I asked him in front of the bird sanctuary's ticket seller.

"Uh-huh," he said, handing me the small bags of birdseed. He adjusted the brim on his baseball cap.

"Dyke time," I said. "Gimme a **D**. Gimme a **Y**. Gimme a **K**. Gimme an **E**."

"Just calm down," he said.

We walked along quietly for a while. It was nice to be out in nature with Chris. It was a crisp winter day. The sun was playing hide-and-seek with the clouds.

Once we got farther along the trail, I opened the bag of birdseed for chickadees. Chris took a handful, opened his palm, and held it up in the air, offering a landing spot for the black-capped chickadees watching in a nearby tree.

With my eyes on the chickadees, I asked quietly, "Did I tell you my friend Lila drew a few birds for my book about Vivian?"

He didn't say anything. After a little while, one of the chickadees landed in his palm and started eating the seeds. Then it flew away . He placed the remaining seeds from his palm on a nearby fence post.

"Chris? Did you hear me?" I asked.

"Yes," he said. "I'm just so tired of talking about Vivian. We always talk about Vivian."

"What? We never talk about Viv," I said. "I haven't mentioned her to you for weeks. Because you don't want me to talk about her. Because you want me to pretend that I'm okay. But I'm still not okay, Chris."

"Look, I'm sorry you're not okay, sis," he said. "I don't want you to be bummed out. I don't get how writing about her can help you move on."

"Move on? If I was having a bad day or a bad week, I could reach out to Viv. Now, she's not here," I said. "I don't have a lot of friends." I paused. A group of quacking ducks approached us, so I opened the duck seed and threw them a couple of handfuls to get them to veer in another direction.

I steered us to a small nook along the trail. I turned to Chris. "Have you had anyone close to you die before? How would you feel if I died? How long would you feel bummed? A few days? A week? A year? My best friend died." I told myself that I wouldn't cry in public. I've done it before and it's never good.

Chris was quiet for a minute. "I know that I'm not the best brother, but I hate seeing you drop out of school and sit in your apartment with your cat all day."

"C'mon," I said. I held up my index finger. "Number one: I didn't drop out of school. I'm taking a leave of absence. I'm going back soon." I made a peace sign with my index and middle fingers. "Number two: Whisk is the cutest cat ever. She is a legend on the internet." I dropped my index finger, so I just had my middle finger in his face now. "Finally, fuck that. You just need to be here for me. That's it. I love you, but don't tell me how to live my life." I put away my middle finger. "Now, let's see some owls, bitch."

"Don't call me a bitch, bitch," he said, cracking a smile.

"When you're a bitch, I'll call you a bitch," I said.

"Whatever," he said.

We walked farther and watched two tiny owls sleeping in the branches of a tree. They were barely visible. A mom asked her kid what the word was for when you stay awake at night and sleep during the day. The kid said, "Nocturnal." A little farther up the trail, we saw two larger owls sleeping in a tree. They were easier to see. People were hooting to try to wake them up. "Hoo hoo." The sleeping owls were not fooled and kept on sleeping. Chris told me these owls were great horned owls, and the tiny ones we'd seen earlier were northern saw-whet owls.

I had no idea that I'd end up listening to so much of the Britpop that Viv loved. Some of it doesn't move me, but there are a few songs that wring me out like a washcloth. "The Trees" by Pulp. "Hermit Crab" by the Wonder Faults. "Sometimes It Hurts" by Tindersticks.

Lately, it's been Suede's "The Wild Ones" that topples me. It's pretty and melancholy and ends with four words sung again and again. "Oh, if you stay." I'd be tempted to nominate "oh" as the most expressive word in the English language. It's versatile enough to convey anguish, confusion, surprise, and ecstasy. It means everything and nothing. "Oh" goes to a place most words can't reach. It's the sound of breathing, the sound of being alive, the sound you make with a lover who knows how to fuck you. "Oh, if you stay." And, of course, it's impossible for me not to think of Viv when I hear the line "on you my tattoo will be bleeding and the name will stain." My fingers trace the tattoo over my heart, the permanent cursive letter V in her handwriting.

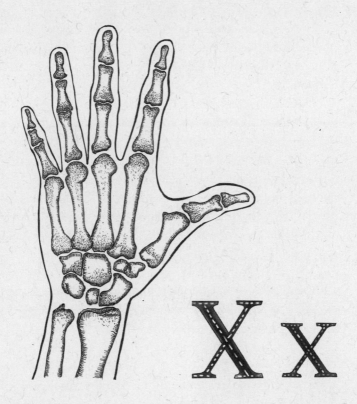

Sadly, there are no characters whose last names start with an **X**. I can't even shoehorn an entry here. Carter Exby, you're just a phonetic tease.

It seems like I'm forever putting **X**'s into boxes.

On my leave of absence form to take an authorized break from grad school, I had to select the type of leave I was requesting. There were five categories. I put an **X** inside the PERSONAL box to indicate that I'd encountered "personal circumstances" that would "significantly interfere" with my studies. I'd also had to write a memo explaining why I would be absent. It was a brief memo.

I just submitted the official form to let people in grad studies know I'd be returning to the journalism program next term. At least now Christopher and my mom will leave me alone.

I also deactivated my online dating profile. Before I could suspend my account, the site asked me to put an X beside the appropriate box to explain why I was leaving. None of the five options explained my departure. I needed an option for OTHER so I could write, "The cute queer sloths on this site are dishearteningly slow at messaging me. And sometimes they vanish." Or maybe I'd channel Viv and put, "Nobody on this glitchy site seems to realize how desirable, loveable, and fuckable I am." In the end, I put an X beside the option reading, "I got too many messages," which suggested that I was being pestered by amorous queers who didn't quite cut the mustard. Not true, but when given a choice I'd prefer to sound picky rather than pathetic.

Dot invited me to karaoke at her favourite place. She got a babysitter for Teddy. When I arrived, she was waiting for me with two shots of Chartreuse. We hugged and clinked glasses and downed the shots. I'd forgotten how herbal and potent it was. She led me to our own little karaoke room. Dot handed me the song list and I quickly discovered why she liked this spot. It specialized in punk and new wave songs.

"Pick a song," she said. "C'mon. Pick. A. Song."

I flipped through the pages. It had been a while since I'd been to karaoke and I was overwhelmed and suddenly nervous to sing in front of her. We'd never been to karaoke together. I asked her to go first, pleaded with her to go first.

She selected a song, took the mic, and launched into "Identity" by X-Ray Spex. She went from standing in place to bouncing around in just a few seconds. It was impossible to take your eyes off her while she sang. She was a whirligig. She was free and having fun. As the song ended, she collapsed into her chair.

"We need more Chartreuse," she said, a little out of breath. "And you need to choose a song, princess."

I chose a song and grabbed the mic. It was "Yes, I'm a Witch" by Yoko Ono. I wasn't that familiar with Yoko until Ruby sat me down one night and introduced me to her music. Her band Vulva Death Grip covered "Yes, I'm a Witch," which should be a contender if we ever have a trans femme international anthem. It's so obscure that I didn't expect to see it at a karaoke joint.

When I finished singing, Dot said, "Yoko Ono? That was SO good. You have to do that one again later, okay?!" I smiled, shrugged, and rolled my eyes. It's the kind of gesture Shirley Temple might have done, but I've heard it's kinda cute when I do it, so I probably do it more often than I should.

We went back and forth singing songs, drinking more Chartreuse. We even sang one duet. Dot said we had to sing the song "Stumblin' In" by Suzi Quatro and Chris Norman. I was confused. It was a cheesy classic rock boy-girl duet from the seventies. But she even got on her knees and said something like, "I beseech you, m'lady." It was weird. I told her I'd do it, but only if I could do the Suzi Quatro part. I'd had a crush on Suzi Quatro from the time I was about ten. I mean, she was cute and wore a leather jacket and leather pants and played a character named Leather. Even when I was in elementary school, I was a little dyke tomboy. Dot agreed, saying she'd never ask me to sing the boy part. It felt surreal singing a corny love duet while locking eyes with my dead friend's sister. I was sure Dot and Viv had probably sung this song into hairbrush microphones together a dozen times.

That was the last song we sang in our private little room. Our time was up. Dot still had another couple hours of babysitting, so we walked to a bar a few blocks away. We shared a cigarette en route. I only smoke once or twice a year and only if I've been drinking. I felt that immediate head-rush, the reason people start smoking in the first place. Dot had quit smoking when she got pregnant with Teddy. But she was an adult and her sister had died and she knew what she needed to keep herself from falling apart. We finished the cigarette and went in. The bar was dingy and bourbon sours were on special. Bourbon sours it was. I ordered mine extra sour.

We sat in a corner with our drinks. "To Viv." We clinked glasses. The drink was delightfully sour.

"I was in love with Viv," I said.

"I knew that," Dot said. "It was pretty obvious."

"Oh, really," I said. "I don't think I really realized it until after she died. Then it hit me. I think she was the love of my life. I know Viv and I would have been a terrible couple. I get that now."

Dot laughed. "Oh my god! I can't even imagine." She shook her head. "I love Viv and I love you, but oh god, yes, you two would have been the worst couple."

She raised her glass. "Worst couple ever," she said. We cheersed to that.

She leaned in and put her face close to mine. "How are you really doing?" she asked softly. "I worry about you working on this book. Don't get me wrong. Viv was awesome. But she was flawed."

I sipped my bourbon sour. It was mostly egg foam at this point.

"Without Viv," I said, "I don't know that I would have made it. She was there for me at the most difficult time in my life. When nobody else was there. She kept me alive." I paused. "I know that we wouldn't have been a good couple and I know that if we'd dated it would have ruined everything. She was attracted to men who weren't good enough for her. Some of them were terrible. They broke her heart in so many places. It's like she had a fucking Humpty Dumpty heart."

·"Yeah," Dot said. "Her heart got broken so many fucking times."

"But somehow she kept putting it back together again. I don't know how she did it. At the time, I thought she was super naive to be so open. Now I think she was super brave. But the way some of these guys treated her was sad as fuck. She was so beautiful and delightful and most of these guys just didn't see that."

"She had a lot of people who loved her," Dot said. "She knew how much you loved her. And in her own way she loved you right back."

"Fuck," I said. "I should be consoling you. Not the other way around."

Dot shook her head. "I'm fine," she said. "I miss her every day, but I'm fine. Teddy makes it hard to wallow."

"Wallow rhymes with swallow," I said. "Sorry. Why the fuck did I say that?"

She laughed. "Because you're channelling your inner Viv. And because we need more drinks."

We ordered one more round of bourbon sours.

Damn you, Jason Bloch. You have no **X** characters and no **Y** characters?! *Macbeth* is quoted repeatedly on *Little Blue*, and I've found myself returning to Shakespeare while writing about the series and about Vivian. And Yorick is one of the absent characters in Shakespeare who stands out for me. As an aside, Yorick would be a great name for a Yorkshire Terrier. Alas, Yorick the Yorkie, a dog of infinite unrest, of most excellent fancy.

Shakespeare, you died 400 years ago, but these lines can make me instantly melancholic and nostalgic: "Here hung those lips that I have kissed I know / not how oft." Unlike

Hamlet and Yorick, I know exactly how oft Viv and I kissed: only once. We were kneeling on the floor sharing a bowl of drunk late-night instant noodles on Viv's coffee table. Somehow, we found ourselves munching on either ends of a long noodle à la Lady and the Tramp. We went with it and when we reached the middle, we started kissing, which is awkward to do when you're also chewing and swallowing noodles. We kept kissing. Then, Viv made a whimpering noise and tried using her nose to nudge the bowl of edamame towards me. It was weird and cute. We made out again, ate more noodles and edamame. We alternated between making out and snacking. Then, we alternated between watching an old movie and making out. Eventually, she fell asleep. I took the quilt from her bedroom and tucked her in on the couch. I biked home and we never made out again or talked about the time we made out.

Frank Ocean appeared on *Late Night with Jimmy Fallon* a few days after publishing his open letter confessing that his first love had been another man. For his television debut, he chose to sing "Bad Religion," a song about that unrequited relationship. After an introduction by Fallon that hyped the early iTunes release of *Channel Orange*, Ocean's first major label album, he appeared onscreen, dressed casually in a headband, unbuttoned long-sleeved shirt, and a white T-shirt. The song starts out slowly. It's framed as a confession to an anonymous Muslim taxi driver. We can tell he's Muslim because after Ocean asks him to "outrun the demons," the driver says "Allahu Akbar" and tells him that he should pray. Ocean's reply makes it clear that the demon he can't elude is his love for a man who can't love him back.

This unrequited love
To me it's nothing but a one-man cult
And cyanide in my Styrofoam cup
I could never make him love me
Never make him love me

There are a dozen songs on *Channel Orange* that Ocean could have sung for his television debut, including one of its five singles. But he chose to sing this vulnerable, intense song, a song where the pronouns couldn't be clearer. In case you missed the queer subtlety of him describing his unrequited love as belonging to a one-man cult, Ocean sings clearly, "I could never make him love me," repeating the line for emphasis.

After singing the last lines of the song, Ocean looks briefly and defiantly at the audience. Then, the string section on stage beside him plays the song's outro. When "Bad Religion" ends, Ocean lifts his head and smiles a young, goofy smile. As he'd said in his open letter earlier that week, "I don't have any secrets I need kept anymore." By writing about Viv and writing about myself, I suspect I'm trying to follow his lead and Viv's lead and get to that place.

L ast night, I found myself reading and rereading the poem "To My Trans Friends Who Have Also Considered Suicide" by Elba Congreve:

Sometimes thinking about it helps.
So go ahead and think about the endless
Ways of untethering yourself and ending it.

But please don't abdicate.

Please don't put down
Your ill-fitting crown.
Please don't renounce everything.

Yes, being resilient exhausts us.
And yes barbs and fists wound us.
And yes the weight and wooze of days
Is at times too much to weather.
And yet.

Enough of us already
Barnacle the ocean floors
And ghost the plateaus
And cloud the skies.

Even if it's out of spite
Even if it's to say "fuck you"
Please try to stay alive.

It's the tiny line "And yet" that gets me. After a litany of things about being trans that are galling, those two words give me hope, somehow. "And yet" reminds me of all the things that give me life. And yet there is art and coffee and friends and cuddling and my cat asleep beside me on the couch.

I've been hesitant to talk about how Viv died, but I think it's important to say that Viv didn't commit suicide. That being said, if you don't already know how she died, I won't disclose the details. We aren't defined by how we happen to die. This is my resistance to most events that only focus on reading the names of trans folks and how they were killed. They weren't martyrs who died for a cause. Trans women of colour are murdered for trying to live their lives. Clearly, there's a value in saying their names, in remembering them.

But I want to know who they were, how they lived, who and what they loved in this world.

Lucas ZITO and Tindra North narrate the baseball episode. She provides most of the levity, while he seems to have perfect knowledge about every baseball game that's ever been played on Little Blue Island. He is as bland as a basket of unsalted fries, except when he accidentally says on air that he's surprised Thurman Park, the "best hitter on the entire island by a country mile," has done "sweet fuck all" in the game. He is immediately apologetic and flustered. Tindra tries to salvage the situation by telling a colourful story about the time Thurman invited her to visit his beehives.

During my shifts at the art gallery gift shop, I went for coffee on most of my breaks. At first, I went to the café right across from the gallery. After a while, I tired of their paltry selection of pastries. I walked into another shop up the street and saw Viv behind the counter. All I remember about the first time I saw her was that she was wearing the perfect T-shirt. It had four words on it in bold letters: HIPS TITS LIPS POWER.

Suddenly, I had a new coffee shop for my mid-shift caffeine jolt. Every time I visited, I'd hope Viv was on duty. She was there most of the time, but I was disappointed when she wasn't. Whenever we interacted, I was sheepish and awkward. A friend once described me as mousy and (even though the word stung at the time) she was mostly right. Viv was naturally charming and flirtatious. She often called me "babe," which made my heart trill. I was dating Ramona at the time and pondering how to be trans and not have my transness upset the apple cart of my life. Viv became the only trans woman I knew, and I barely knew her. But I thought about her every day and knew that I wanted what she had.

After countless visits to the coffee shop, I finally managed to screw my courage to the sticking place one wintry afternoon.

"What can I get you, babe?" Viv asked.

"I think I'm trans," I blurted.

It was a slow day in the shop, and no one was within earshot.

"Oh, wow. That's ... that's the best news." She smiled. "Are you a hugger?" she asked.

I nodded. She came around the counter and gave me a long, slow hug.

When she let me go, she said, "Good thing I wore my cry-proof mascara today." She laughed. "Nobody wants to be served by a trans raccoon."

She got behind the counter again. "Whew. Okay. Let me give you a drink on the house to celebrate."

"No, it's okay. It's not a big deal."

"Uh, yes, it is. What do you want? It's gonna be free. So choose well, babe."

When I ordered my usual Americano, she was visibly disappointed.

"So predictable," she said. "Sigh."

I shrugged and rolled my eyes exaggeratedly, trying to distract her from noticing that I was blushing.

"Can I have a name?" she asked. She held a marker beside the paper coffee cup.

There were no other customers in the shop, so I was confused. "Uh, what?"

"Well," she said, "I don't wanna call you the wrong name. What should I call you?"

"I don't know," I said. I had a couple of names that I was using online, but neither of them felt quite right. "I'm still thinking about a name. Sorry."

She studied me with her marker poised. After a while, she smiled, nodded to herself, and jotted a name on the cup.

"What did you write?" I asked.

She shook her head. "You'll see. It's one of the best names."

After pulling a double shot of espresso and adding hot water, she handed me the cup.

She'd written the name "Zelda" on it.

I liked the name. "Why Zelda?" I asked.

She shrugged. "Why not Zelda? Name a better name."

I reddened, again.

Zelda. I loved the letter Z. Years ago, I'd vaguely known a girl named Zosia whose name I'd always adored. One of my online names was Eliza, but it didn't feel quite right.

"I think you've got me," I said.

Viv smiled.

Zelda was a name that never would have occurred to me, but somehow it felt like a name I might be able to inhabit.

I walked over to the cream-and-sugar station. As I was heading out the door, Viv appeared and handed me a piece of paper. The paper read *text me* and had her phone number and name on it.

———

At your funeral, I didn't say anything and I've always regretted it. I owe you a eulogy.

Oh, Viv. I always thought you would die before me. You were willing to take chances that I wasn't, to do things I wouldn't even contemplate. Your past was darker, your ghosts more insistent. You were unshuttered. You nuzzled life. I had a crush on you the size of Greenland. You were an effervescent badass. I miss you. Dot misses you. Teddy misses you. Everyone who loved you or knew you misses you. I'm still melancholic as fuck and I'll probably always have a splinter of sadness that just won't leave me. But I'm keeping shards of you in the world by thinking about you, talking about you, writing about you. The joy of having known you is starting to paint over the pain of having lost you. And when I miss you most, I can absorb myself in something you adored. Suede. *Little Blue.* A houndstooth trench coat. And, voila, to some small degree, there you are with me. Just like your tattoo of the Bride of Frankenstein. "She's alive! Alive!"

You were wild and beautiful and alive. And I still love you with my queer little heart.

ACKNOWLEDGEMENTS

This book was written while living as an uninvited guest on the unceded ancestral territories of the kʷikʷəƛ̓əm (Kwikwetlem), xʷməθkʷəy̓əm (Musqueam), Sḵwx̱wú7mesh (Squamish), and səlílwətaʔɬ (Tsleil-Waututh) Nations.

Thanks to all the trans, Two-Spirit, non-binary, and gender-defiant folks I'm fortunate to have in my life, particularly Gwen, Jessica, Kay, and Mary Ann.

Thanks to all the trans writers, queer writers, and racialized writers whose work keeps me afloat.

Thanks to Tom, Trish, and Zoey, who generously took time from their own work to support mine.

Thanks to Kevin at LOKI for this book's brilliant cover.

Thanks to Onjana, illustrator/poet/friend extraordinaire.

Thanks to Ashley and Oliver at Metonymy for taking a chance on my strange manuscript and for your perceptiveness, your thoughtfulness, and your openness. Thanks also for your ongoing dedication to trans and queer writers and readers.

Thanks to beloved friends, family, felines, and partners in crime, particularly Nikki, Edith Irene, Shannon, Doreen, Nu, Ania, Baharak, Chantal, Travis, Julian, Ryan, Pique, Ramona, Aggie, Ava, Huluu, and DCB.

ABOUT THE AUTHOR

Hazel Jane Plante is a queer trans librarian and writer. *Little Blue Encyclopedia (for Vivian)* is her first novel.

She currently lives in Vancouver on the unceded ancestral territories of the xʷməθkʷəy̓əm (Musqueam), Sḵwx̱wú7mesh (Squamish), and səlílwətaʔɬ (Tsleil-Waututh) Nations.

ALSO AVAILABLE FROM

METONYMY PRESS

Dear Twin
Addie Tsai

nîtisânak
Lindsay Nixon

Lyric Sexology Vol. 1
Trish Salah

Fierce Femmes and Notorious Liars: A Dangerous Trans Girl's Confabulous Memoir
Kai Cheng Thom

Small Beauty
jiaqing wilson-yang

She Is Sitting in the Night: Re-visioning Thea's Tarot
Oliver Pickle